The Shadow Knows

Other Books by David Madden

FICTION

The Beautiful Greed
Cassandra Singing

LITERARY CRITICISM

Wright Morris
Tough Guy Writers of the Thirties (Editor)
Proletarian Writers of the Thirties (Editor)
The Poetic Image in Six Genres

THE SHADOW KNOWS

Stories by David Madden

LOUISIANA STATE UNIVERSITY PRESS □ BATON ROUGE

*F*or my son Blake

"The Shadow Knows" first appeared in *Kentucky Writing;*
"Lone Riding" and "Love Makes Nothing Happen" in *South-
west Review*; "The Pale Horse of Fear" in *Twigs*; "The Day
the Flowers Came" in *Playboy*; and "No Trace" in *The
Southern Review.*

Copyright © 1963, 1966, 1968, 1969, 1970 by David Madden
Library of Congress Catalog Number: 78–108593
SBN Number: 8071–0929–0
Louisiana State University Press
Printed in the United States of America
By Thos. J. Moran's Sons, Inc.
Designed by Jules McKee

Contents

54456

The Shadow Knows

Lone Riding

LONE faced CORBIN STONECIPHER'S JUNKYARD. GOOD PAY FOR SCRAP. The lop-jawed gate of iron and wire hung open. A black-cindered, rutted driveway led into the debris. Smoke rolled tightly out of an iron pipe chimney on the roof of a narrow leaning shack inside the gate. On a billboard above the shack, morning glare bleached a Lucky Strike poster almost white. From a lamppost dangled a new globe. The rock-shattered pieces of the old one lay on the ground. Gran'daddy blamed Blackie. In the middle of the junkyard, a white picket fence surrounded Gran'daddy's house. Stripped mimosa trees, freshly whitewashed, stood in front of the house, where late roses withered on the trellises that framed the porch.

Walking toward a block-long, ten-feet-high stack of grimy batteries, Lone raised dust that coated his boots. Beyond the batteries, a crane dipped its head.

Gran'daddy Stonecipher was lowering a crashed blue Buick, dripping dust. Six feet from a pile of cars, he let it fall and crash on top of a pug-nosed milk truck. The door on the driver's side swung open. Something sparked it, and first smoke, then fire, rose from the heap.

The door in the cab of the crane swung open and Gran'daddy jumped six feet to the ground. Wiping his hands on his coveralls, smeared with sweat, grease, oil, and grit, he looked at Lone from under a tight-fitting cap, the bill coned like that of a duck.

"See that steering shaft? Went straight as hell right through his speeding guts." Through the veil of smoke, Lone saw a blotch of blood on the upholstery. Straw and springs bulged out of the gashed leather. "Had to blow-torch him out. Didn't hurt none though, cause he was already shoveling coal in hell."

Gran'daddy leaned against the stack of batteries, one short arm flung behind his back, the other out stiff, as if to keep the batteries from falling on him. The light flickering up his chest and over his grimy face, he watched the car burn. On the charred scrap heap, it could smolder for days without spreading.

"You at it early, ain't you?"

"Early for Christians," said Gran'daddy, squinting up at Lone, the bright morning sun making his eyelids quiver, "late for hoodlums."

"Say, Gran'daddy, how 'bout my 'sickle?"

"You can't have *my* 'sickle."

"Now, you better not've touched my *'sickle*."

Since he had grown taller than Gran'daddy, Lone was usually embarrassed to stand close to him, but now he *wanted* to look down on him.

"Gonna touch it a couple times with a sledgehammer d'reckly."

"Damn it, where'd you hide it?"

"Talk like that'll get your face slapped for you. Yonder it hangs—over your shoulder."

Lone turned, looking up. A black crane, its hook snagged in the spokes, held the motorcycle high. Above a cluster of wrecked and rusted motorcycles, Lone's bright red one looked lynched, but still alive.

"You ain't about to bury *my* sickle in this graveyard!"

"Can't you tell when a body's trying to take care of

you? You and that pack you run with wrecked twelve dollars' worth of damage in that drive-in last night. Now your uncle Troy could a forced the *money* out of you, but he wanted to hurt and help you at the same time."

"So he slipped up in the yard last night and stole my 'sickle right from under my window." Lone reached in his jacket pocket, brought out seven one-dollar bills and a five, and held them out. "Now ease it down."

Gran'daddy jerked his cap down over his eyes. "You just have to keep trying, don't you?"

"What?"

He cocked back his cap, showing thin, pale-yellow hair going gray. "You want me to have to haul it in off the highway?"

"What *else* do you pray for?"

"God don't need to be asked. He's got it down in the book for soon."

"Well, turn loose of it, if you're so sure you'll get it back."

"Look at that Buick burn! Labor Day they'll be twenty or thirty drug in here from the Nashville, Asheville, Oak Ridge, and Louisville highways. I'm sure of *that*, son."

"I ain't your son. Troy's *your* son—Knoxville's public enemy cop number one."

"Still want that face of yours slapped?"

Lone stared a moment into Gran'daddy's face. Grit had worked into every pore in his skin, but his keen blue eyes gave his face a clean, open look. When he bugged his eyes and pinched his mouth, as he did now, Lone had to look down. He looked at the splayed-open hands that had manhandled every scrap of junk inside the fence.

"All I want's my 'sickle."

"Take it. I'll wait. I'll pick it up off the highway some

early morning . . . It all ends up here!" Stomping three times with the same foot, he raised dust, a violent blend of grease, soot, dirt, acid, and rust. "The good Lord had something on his mind when he stuck my junkyard in the middle of Knoxville. And who you reckon got that new superhighway routed through your house, but made it miss my junkyard? Someday I'll junk this whole town. And you with it, trash of the family that you are." He looked at Lone as if he saw some picture of the future. "Else you overcome the devil in you, and throw off that Blackie Weaver that's took hold of you and turned you deaf to—"

He seized Lone's hand and swung him around behind the stack of batteries. As Lone opened his mouth to curse him, the Buick's gas tank exploded. Flames shooshed up, curled above the stack. A vomit of black smoke thinned around the neck of the crane. As they stepped around the corner to view the wreckage, Lone eased his hand out of Gran'daddy's.

". . . like salvation, son. A way. A way to see. And seeing will do it. See man in the muck, then see Christ on Calvary. I drop 'em just right on purpose to get that. I want 'em to burn, to show anybody standing around how it ought to end. They come in here, son, the blood still wet—if it was a fire already, the skin burned into the *up*holstery. You want to know what that does? Makes a man see. If anybody was to ask you what man has come to, you show him this. Gather it all in and pile it all up and hammer it all down and ship it all out—feel like you're cleaning up the corruption that makes this godforsaken city run. Well, it runs, now don't it? Runs itself out, runs itself down, runs itself into a intersection right when another one's doing the same on white lightnin'. And when they dig us all up, there'll be the history of Knoxville inside these gates, layer by layer." Then he laughed. "They's something about seven o'clock in the blamed morning . . ."

Lone had it on his tongue to ask him, "But ain't they no love in it?" when Gran'daddy gave his shoulder a pat, and that was his answer: Lone.

Gran'daddy climbed into the cab of the crane and, with squeaks and clanks that put Lone's teeth on edge, eased the motorcycle down until its hind wheel touched the soft black dirt. As Lone pulled the hook out of the bent spokes, the motorcycle's full weight sunk in his arms, pulling him to his knees.

"Listen now, Lone, I don't want your money. If you can work in that knitting mill with your momma all summer just to save up a hundred dollars to buy a wrecked motorsickle, you can work off that twelve dollars to get it back. I don't want to eat into your school time, cause I know your momma's got your future mapped out on that high-school diploma. But on Saturday, a dollar a time, till you grow to love it. You know, look at it one way, they's something about junk that thrills a body's soul."

"That Blackie sure knows how to take a piece of junk like this was and make it purr like a tomcat between your legs on the open highway."

"Your momma talks about you turning out a doctor and healing your poor little sister of the rheumatic fever, but *I'm* saying this place'll make a preacher of you. Start in tomorrow, Lone."

"Gran'daddy, I tell you, I be glad to work off what I owe you, but tomorrow—"

"Forget it."

"Now don't take it that way . . ."

"Take it, hell. *You* take it. Take it on out of here." Pulling down hard on the bill of his cap, he turned in the powdery dust. "Pass on what filth the sewers of this town has cut loose in you," he said, walking toward the open cab door of the crane.

Lone slapped into a swarm of gnats with the back of his hand, swung his leg over the motorcycle, and mounted.

Coasting into the yard, his tires slid on the dewy grass, and he let the motorcycle slur and throw him. The rear wheel pinned him to the grass from ankle to knee. He let it lie, let the pain throb. From the black shapes of persimmons and the oval leaves, drops of dew fell on his face, clinked on the fender. Evening clouds had thinned and passed, and the stars were hard and clear, and he felt summer go out of him and out of the earth in one moment. It would be autumn in the morning.

He turned his head in the damp grass, and the glow of the weak light in the room he shared with Cassie fell across the porch. The light meter on the wall beside the mailbox whirred and clicked like a pistol cocking. Within reach, an Atlas truck tire hung from a chain. He gave it a little shove and watched it swing. He listened. No sounds came from the house. Only the tick of dewdrops on the fender that cut into his leg, the click of steel as the motorcycle cooled.

Struggling out from under the motorcycle, he stood up and limped into the road, trying to jar feeling back into his numb leg. The leaves of the kudzu vines that crawled thickly over the side of the ridge and hunched over the trees hissed in the wind like skittering lizards. Feeling the pain come back, he limped into the grass toward the porch, letting the motorcycle lie. It was over. The night of speed, when he turned the earth with his handlebars. He'd have to go in. And listen.

On the bottom step, he glanced over at Momma's window. The yellow shade was drawn within a foot of the sill—the cord and finger-loop swung slightly. As though she had jerked it down a minute ago. Lone started up, but stopped as she passed the window in her pink slip. Along her ribs, wear and wash had pulled the rayon thin. He was ashamed. Before quitting the mill, he should have bought her a strong new slip instead of the butterfly broach. The butterfly to soothe her when she smelled moonshine on his breath.

She sat on the bed, sideways, with her hands on her knees, her head tilted back so she could slip off the hair net and release her long brown hair. She closed her eyes very softly. And sighed. He felt the weariness of her body in his own.

When Lone's foot landed noiselessly on the next step Momma looked up. Her finger suddenly at her lips, her other hand made a warning for him to go back into the yard. He listened: Coot on the back porch, fumbled opening of the screen door, rattle of the knob in the door, sudden opening and banging of the door against the kitchen wall. "Out, you mangy—out! I said, *git!*" The screen slammed. "Quit tormenting me. Can't I go nowhere 'thout'n a pack of dogs drooling all over my heels? Strike for the barn where y'b'long!" When he shoved the door shut, the house shook till Lone felt vibrations faintly in his boots. Then a swaying silence. "I gotta see my youn'un . . ." Coughing, mumbling, he moved across the kitchen, a sudden sharp scrape as he stumbled over a chair.

On the porch, Lone put his hand in the mailbox, expecting a notice from the draft board ordering him to report for a physical: a sediment of rust in the bottom. Sniffing the rank flakes on his fingertips, he went to the wall and moved carefully toward the window, avoiding the swing chains. Last night, he had stumbled up to the attic, like climbing a washboard, and awakened his daddy out of a deep sleep to tell him the barn was afire. A friendly joke. One that made Coot stomping mad. This morning, Coot had awakened Lone out of a deep sleep to tell him some-one had stolen his motorcycle. By the time he had con-vinced Lone that his Uncle Troy had confiscated it, the damage had been done. Things had been said. Things not easily taken back.

Putting his ear to the clapboards, he felt the inevitability of return. Coot's shoulders bumped and scraped the wall as he staggered down the hallway. He whispered so loud-ly that the dogs, slinking back up to the barn, probably heard him: "Cassie? Cassie, you awake, child? H'it's you' daddy, honey. Wanna come in and set a spell and talk a while."

Lone glanced in the window. The blanket wrapped tightly around her, Cassie sat at the foot of the bed, her back against the faintly damp wall, her green, feverish eyes wide open. As the door opened, the rusty hinges whining, she fell, turning as she tipped, and landed dead-weight on the bed, twisted in the covers, her back to the door, her face toward the bottom rail and the only win-dow.

"You playlike you asleep but you hear even more'n I say. You hear what I don't say, too. Tomorrow you'll sing about it when ever'body's gone. Charlotte's in the fact'ry, Lone's in school, and Coot's on the ridge with the hounds, and only you and the flies are home, and the cock-roaches listen and clap their hands, cause they know what *you* know. That they'll inherit this house one fine day." Coot untwisted the lid of a mason jar, slurped, and let out his breath in a gust. Looking through the window, Lone saw Coot at the foot of Cassie's bed, leaning over the bottom railing, lifting a long, full strand of her blond hair. Lone felt a faint pull in his own scalp. "Soft, soft, God-awful soft . . . Clap their hands and listen and wait . . . rolling over and over in the foggy, foggy soot, down in the valley of death. Lone!" Coot slapped the wall. "You get on home, you hear? . . . Good night, goodnight, ladies, I have to leave you now." He stumbled down the hallway. Knocking over chairs in the kitchen, he climbed the stairs to the attic. "Brrrr! H'it's turning cold as a witch's tit!" When he hit the steps, he sounded like a big man.

"Some night when he sleeps up yonder I look to see his foot come right through that ceiling," said Momma, whispering with the huskiness of half-sleep as Lone walked into her bedroom. Seeing that, Lone laughed. Momma bounced and scooted along the edge of the bed to her night table and tapped a sleeping pill out of the bottle. She swallowed one and dashed some water after it. "I don't even listen to him when he gets that way. Poor ol' soul. Mumble, mumble."

"Since when did you take to pills?"

"Since you took to that contraption!" She slapped the bottle of pills on the loose-jointed night table; they popped out like jumping beans. Lone slumped to his knees, and Momma turned on the light and bent over, and they picked them up. "You're the only healthy one left, Lone. Be thankful *you* overcame that blamed fever." Lone stood up. Pulling Momma up with one hand, he handed her the bottle with the other. "You know what I sniffed when we were down there on our hands and knees, don't you?"

"Just a few dabs . . ."

"You staying away from that Travis girl, ain't you? Say! Gypsy Travis can cause you a world of grief. She comes of pure trash that lives off the welfare."

"Well, no need to act proud, Momma. People call this whole edge of Knoxville 'Welfare Creek.' "

"McDaniels and Stonaciphers was here before that. Now you weren't *with* her tonight, were you?"

"I'm tired, Momma. I been riding from Tennessee to hell and back since daybreak. Gotta sleep *some*time." He gazed at the wrinkles on the edge of Momma's bed where she had sat. "My bones are creaking, I'm so tired."

"Well, if you'd treat this house like it was more than a flophouse between one strange city and another, you'd—"

"Reckon I've turned out a hoodlum to most people, but maybe if I lit out for the South Pole . . ."

"You can't take a step without that Blackie Weaver, and he'd stick in Knoxville the rest of his life if he thought it'd torment *me*."

"Aw, Momma, people throw off on Blackie like he's some snake the flood washed up. What you expect of somebody that come from a momma like Mrs. Weaver? And with less of a daddy than *I've* got. I reckon he turns to me like I's his little brother or something."

"I reckon it was your big brother put that stink on your breath."

"Momma, I swore I'd never bring the smell of it in your house, and I'm sorry. I hoped to sneak by you."

"Well, hop in bed and sleep it off."

"Any place to lay my head . . ."

"Lord knows, I'll no sooner put mine down than the alarm clock'll wring it off. And I got to get you off to school to boot. Lord, if I could just get my mind off my worries..."

"Be like *me*. Forget."

She patted his leather sleeve with one hand and pulled the light chain with the other. The brass clinking against the globe, she said, "Night, night, honey, sleep tight."

Then he remembered that for almost half an hour he *had* forgotten. Forgotten that Frank Burnett lay in the city morgue with a tag around his big toe.

He groped for his mother's hand in the dark, about to speak, but "Frank" caught in his throat like a sharp popcorn hull. And she had turned to the bed. It whined under her. He crossed the hall to the bedroom where Cassie lay. Wide awake.

He slapped his cap over a nail beside the window and unzipped his jacket, a loud rasping. Taking off the jacket and throwing it over the gutless console radio in the corner, he felt like a stripper, knowing that in her mind Cassie picked it up and slipped it over her own thin shoulders. He unzipped his pants and flung them over the foot of the cot, the buckle clanking against the metal frame. He sat heavily on the edge. Cassie lay in the brass bed, her face toward him, lids closed, but eyes wide open on the picture of him in her mind. He sat very still a few moments, sighing deeply, then, grunting, pulled the boots off and set them neatly, side by side, at the head of the cot.

A motorcycle rumbled on the other side of the hill, revved loud at the top, and swooped down. The light bounced over Lone, swinging his shadow along the wall, bending it over the ceiling. The light paused a moment, aimed straight through the window, casting a shadow of the swing chains, two overlapping triangles suspended by two lengths, on the dahlia-patterned wall. As he turned to glance through the window, the light swung out of the room. Everybody else crawling into bed: old Blackie still chasing his tail. Then the headlight dipped over the hill.

He crawled in under the covers, and, too weary to reach up and pull down the shade, threw his arm over his eyes to keep out the moonlight. Across the hall, momma coughed and turned in her bed.

He waited for Cassie to speak. She lay in his clothes in the big bed, the past churning up in her like flowers that she would lay over him until the fumes put him to sleep. He turned his head from the window, where leaves lay curled on the sill, toward the bed, and his eyes met Cassie's unlidded, glazed stare. "Lone, honey, you remember . . . ?" No, he didn't. And he didn't want to. But he kept his mouth shut. ". . . the times when me and you would sit in that old orange *pro*duce truck in the field just 'fore dark, eating blackberries till our teeth and lips turned from blue to black, and we'd kiss the window to see it stain . . . ? Oh, and 'member, honey, how it got so cold sometimes we'd put our tongues on the brass railing of the bed and to break loose took the skin off . . . ? Reminds me of those pictures in National Geographics of the valley of ten thousand smokes in Alaska where we always wanted to go . . . And I can still taste the jack rocks in my mouth, the time you stuck a crayon in your ear to disappear, like that magician at the Bijou . . . Remember that summer I had such a long good spell and roamed every inch of Knoxville, and Coot turned up missing and it was me found him? Over around Vine Street that's thick as Buzzard's Roost with niggers—in the basement of one of those old-timey houses, marked with a yellow X now for where the freeway's plowing through, and he was laid up in a dark room full of niggers, drunk and unconscious, and they had stripped him and were playing poker for who got his clothes, and talking about him like he was the sweetest old boy they ever came across."

What made her remember these things *tonight*? What reminded her? That, as much as *what* she remembered, made him shiver. He lit a cigarillo. Instead of letting her frighten him with the past, he would thrill her with the present. Let his own voice and a cigarillo put him to sleep. First, he let her finish. "Yeah, I remember . . . Did you hear us tonight?"

"Momma said you ripped by the revival tent to torment her. I can always tell your motor from the others. When you all stop quick, I see the black marks on the cement, and the tires smoke when they scream around curves, and people look out their windows, frowning, cussing, some of 'em laughing. I heard you shoot onto the highway and through a tunnel of big trees, and the moon leaks silver coins on the black macadam, and you all race between ghostly fences, that yellow stripe ripping between you, and horses grazing lift their faces, them lonely eyes, and cold, dripping noses, and stare at the blurry speed and the smoke, and they stamp the frozen ground and whinny, the noise makes them so nervous. Then it begins to snow."

"You got it all mixed up. Ain't been any snow yet, and we didn't go out to the country." But tomorrow, riding in the procession to the cemetery, he would have to slow down and try to separate what *she* had told *him* from what he was now going to tell *her*.

"Tell me about it, Lone." Hearing her sit up in bed, he turned over on his stomach, rose on his elbows, and looked at her. Through the dust-streaked silicone of his goggles, her eyes looked at him.

"Give me them goggles, Cassie. I needed them damn things all night."

"Tell me, and I'll give 'em back."

"You stole 'em from me!"

"I never. They slipped out of your jacket and I kinda sat on them."

"Hand 'em over."

"Then tell it. *Ever'thing.*"

"Now, Cassie." Across the hall, Momma was wide awake, straining to hear every word. "You let your brother get some sleep."

Realizing he wouldn't be able to sleep at all until he had told her, he turned over on his back again and stared through the window at the moon in the buckeye tree. "Frank is—" A pack of dogs that roamed the ridge wild barked, crossing Oak Ridge highway to get onto Sharp's Ridge again. No, Frank wasn't dead *yet.* "I made Gran'-daddy fork over my 'sickle early this morning, then I put in some time at school 'cause I didn't want them calling Momma at the factory. We met at the quarry, and Cowboy was the first one, on his blue and white that had a sort of sick cough when it idled, but Blackie fixed it for him. Then here come Bluetail on his zebra. Then Gypsy and Junebug come down the railroad and up the path."

"Wearing blue jeans and—"

"Now, Cassie, don't you start that on me. Hush. Gypsy was wearing a wide white band in her hair, just like I like. Sets off hair blacker'n any gypsy. So there we all were when Blackie rode into the quarry and pulled a bottle out of his jacket. That Buzzard Roost bootlegger never turns him loose without tucking one in his saddlebags. We killed it, then lit a rag for the fair.

"We was scorching the highway about to cross the viaduct when I caught sight of a detective's squad car coming toward us past the carbarn in front of a Chilhowee Park bus. It was Troy, sure as the world, so we greased some lightnin' up McCalla and ducked him."

"And somebody sitting in the back of the bus saw your taillights fade up the hill past Swan's bakery," said Cassie.

"Will you all quit that whispering in yonder, Cassie?" said Momma. "That boy has to get up for school in the morning."

"It's *me* talking, Momma. We'll hush." He waited until he felt Momma's sleep was part of the silence.

"And Gypsy's breath on your neck," said Cassie, "and her arms tight around your chest."

"They wouldn't let us in the fairgrounds with our motorsickles. And everybody got mad. We had to park seven blocks away in a residential area on McCalla where the cops might tow them in. When we jumped the fence, the man hired to patrol it came at us with one of those canes they all carry to beat back such as us, the old codger.

"More people at the fair tonight than ever I saw. We were all hot in our jackets, but we kept them on. People made way for us. All those black jackets and caps and black boots, I reckon. Except Cowboy had on those boots with the scrawlie designs, and a fancy stitched shirt. Even Bluetail looked like something you better step aside for. We all looked clean and sharp as could be, jackets greased. Going through Happy Holler on the way, we got the notion to buy us all a pair of white gloves in one of those cheap department stores to see how it would look. People staring at us, we felt it was partly the gloves.

"We target shot a while and batted a few and rode the silver streak that a guy we know and's afraid of Blackie let us ride free till we got almost sick, and at the Dodgems we jumped from one car to another, trying to run down the ticket man when he told us to stop, and most of the people got out over near the fence and the narrow runway, so we had the pit to ourselves, except for this one little kid that Cowboy finally got to crying, and I told him to knock it the hell off. And then we threw baseballs at the red gadget that dunks the white guy made up silly to look like a nigger. We rowed out on the lake and raced the ducks, and then hung around the skating rink. Didn't skate. Just stood behind the green wooden barrier and watched, drinking Orange Crushes. No place like a skating rink—the music like merry-go-round music and the smell of the floor like a bunch of parked, idling motorsickles, and the all kinds of looks on their faces, traveling that floor, waltzing backwards and swinging into dips and spinning and pumping up speed again. We always seem quiet and still in there, and watch all the good ones until they get tired. Up across the lake on the hillside we strolled through the exhibition hall, and Junebug plucked a prize rose from a vase, and we ambled on into the stock pens where they were showing the animals.

"Well the Hellhounds couldn't sit still long, so we headed for the midway rides again, looking for the motorsickle stunt riders. We found 'em by the high wire fence, next to Margo the Snake Girl's tent. It's just a big barrel-like thing with steps leading up to a circle walkway where you can look down into the pit at the motorsickles going around and around. On the platform outside, a barker was giving it hell, and a cyclist sat astride his 'sickle, gunning the motor to whip up your interest. It was Frank Burnett."

"But didn't he quit the gang and run off from home?"

"He did. And took up with this outfit at the fair in Indiana. And there he was back. I never knew him that he didn't talk of running off from home. So when Blackie riding around so pretty made us all want to take up motorsickles, Frank found a way. Just rode with us a few weeks. Then one day he didn't show up at the rock quarry, and the next we knew was tonight, seeing him up there drowning out the whole midway with that muffler, banging it off like a shotgun.

"He didn't see us. Even when we all collected right below the front wheel, looking up at him. Seemed like he sighted straight between the handlebars over the crowd's heads at nothing. Blackie reached up and grabbed Frank's ankle and shook his leg, grinning. Frank didn't act too tickled to see us. You could tell deep down he was teed off to end up back in Knoxville so quick. He shook off Blackie's hand and let the motor idle and said, 'Let's watch that, Blackie.' Not smart. He never did like to talk smart or even show off.

"The old man barking the show leaned down and asked Frank what the trouble was, and Frank smiled finally and said, 'Nothing. Just some old friends of mine.' But he still didn't look at the rest of us, just Blackie. Then we played like we were above it all, and listened to the barker. He was good. He pulled 'em away from the Snake Girl and the freak show and even the girlie show, looking each person in the crowd right in the eye.

"Then Frank got up and went inside, through a little door in the side of the barrel, and we were first in line for tickets. Me and Gypsy walked with Blackie around the outside rail and looked out over the fairgrounds at the rides and shows and people all churned up. I wanted to be around a place like that all the time. I wanted to be down there in that pit, walking around or just sitting, waiting for my partner to finish."

"Let me be the headless girl." Cassie made a musical sound deep in her throat, imitating the background music for a monster movie. "We could run off together."

"Hush. The people crowded around this thick wire barrier, waiting for them to get going. Then from the loudspeaker right over my head, the barker said, 'Okay, folks, it's time now to place the act on the wall.'" The motors roared up out of the pit and the people stepped back a little. I squeezed through and pressed up against the wire.

"Frank had on a brown leather flier's helmet, a purple silk shirt, and black puff-legged riding pants and light brown knee boots. He looked up casually at the people like he didn't *give* a damn, while he got as much noise as he could get out of his 'sickle in that hollow barrel before he let it roll. 'Keep your eye on Lightnin' Bill, folks. He's the newest sensation in the profession. The midway offers no spectacle to equal what you're about to see.' I thought he meant the tall, skinny guy with the mustache and buck teeth, but Frank must've changed his name when he changed his home. The other rider went out the side door and shut it. Frank took it slow at first, like he was trying to pick which street to take at an intersection. But the only way to go was up and around, since with the door shut, *out* was part of the wall. Frank was alone. And the way he pulled down his goggles and rubbed his wrists, wrapped in leather, that seemed to be how he wanted it. Then he started up the wall, going until he was parallel to the floor, coming up at the white line. The women screamed bloody murder. Frank was always so homely he never was much with girls, but the screaming seemed to be part of what he felt. He put his hands behind his head. He rode sidesaddle. He stood up, and stuck straight out from the side of the barrel. Then Frank folded his arms and put his feet up on the handlebars. Had us all playing statues, we was so hypnotized. One girl stayed leaning over the edge. Only her eyes moved. Right with the motorsickle. A long-stemmed rose drooping in her hand—made of crepe paper that she won in that fish game by the Dodgems. Her mouth opened in awe, and I saw she had a cavity between her two front teeth, but she had the prettiest hair.

"When the other guy did his act, and when it was over, Frank walked around on the wooden mats with a hand mike and asked for donations for the special fund, because the work's dangerous. I pitched down a quarter and Bluetail said, 'Can't you read?' and I looked at the sign he was pointing to: DO NOT THROW FOREIGN OBJECTS INTO THE PIT WHILE MOTORSICKLE IS IN MOTION. I laughed and watched Blackie toss something down. Frank went over to it, but when he saw it was a war penny, he stepped over it and looked back up at him over his shoulder like he didn't expect nothing better from Blackie.

"As we came down the steps, the old snaggle-toothed barker asked us how we liked the show.

" 'Hell, anybody can do *that* stuff,' said Blackie. 'But what I love to hear is *you*, talking over that mike. Reckon could *I* try it?'

" 'Hell, man, cut loose!' The barker handed Blackie the mike and stepped back.

"So we stood in the crowd and watched Blackie clown

it up. But *he* was good, too. Can't nobody say he didn't look the part. Frank stayed inside, and the buck-toothed rider came out of the barrel, counting some change in his hand, and sat out front, revving his motor. Then he went in, and the girl with the cavity and the paper rose was the first in the ticket line.

"The show started up again. You could tell Blackie loved the sound of it when he said, 'And now, folks, we're gonna place the act on the wall.' When he gave Frank's real name and said Frank was just a beginner and don't laugh at him, we all laughed and danced around on the sawdust, imagining how mad that must of made Frank. He'd already begun when we went back up to watch him.

"Just as we got up to the railing, I saw that girl toss the rose into the barrel. Later, she said she got the idea from a bullfight movie and thought she'd try it. Said she liked Frank's looks. Well, the way he looked when they pulled the motorsickle off him was like a panther had been let in."

Lone heard Momma's bare feet on the sill of the door. "Do I have to *beg* you all?" Lone and Cassie looked at her a second, then Lone rolled over and pulled the covers over his head. "I've stood this ever' night since that motorsickle *come*. Now keep them traps *shut*." She came in and Lone heard her coax Cassie to the head of the bed and tuck her in. Tight. Then she closed their door and, faintly, hers.

Lone was almost asleep when Cassie spoke in his ear, her breath hot. "Then what?" Wrapped in the quilt, she had squatted on the floor at the head of the cot, her hip against his boots, her ear on a level with his mouth if he turned. To get rid of it, he turned and whispered into her ear, her wispy blond hair tickling his nose and mouth.

"Nothing much. We rode behind the ambulance to General Hospital. They rolled Frank out of the emergency room, and while they waited for the elevator, we went over to him, and June and Gypsy started to cry. 'It was the chance I took,' said Frank. 'Ain't nothing to weep over.' We sat down on a bench, like a church bench, along the wall, and watched the elevator indicator as he went up. It stopped only a second on the fifth floor, then started down. The doors opened, and it was Frank, the sheet over his face."

"I used to lean out the window and watch you and him smoke Indian cigars under the Indian cigar tree."

"That's all, Cassie." He snubbed the cigarillo in the motorcycle hubcap he used as an ashtray. "And please don't bring it up tomorrow. Forget it."

"Then why'd you tell me?"

"Night night, Cassie."

"Night night, Lone. Sleep tight and don't let the bedbugs bite." She kissed him under his ear and went back to her bed, and he pulled the blanket up to his eyes.

A train passed below the meadow. They listened together. Lone inhaled deeply. It came out in a long shudder. Then he was dead to the world. No dreams. Ever, anymore. A blank. Like the tar paper roof of the coal house in the moonlight where beads of dew were forming.

The World's One Breathing

*M*cLAIN wakes. The motor is idling, the bus is shuddering, and he is startled to see old men rising from seats in the front. "Could have wiped out every one of them," says the driver, "in a single swipe." Three seats behind him, McLain rises to look through the front window. "They must be *living* right."

"Where's *this*, driver?"

"Almost to Truckston."

"Why are we stopping?"

"Ask whoever's driving that rolling whorehouse."

McLain sees now that the bus has stopped alongside an outmoded mauve Cadillac that straddles the double yellow line, the wipers still flapping, the headlights dimming out. Five men stand around it, getting into position to push. An overloaded coal truck, a pickup, and two other cars are parked east and west along the road.

Most of the old men are out of their seats, clustered around the driver, trying to get a good view. McLain glances at them. When he fell asleep, the bus had been empty. The sudden presence of ten or eleven old men surrounding him makes him nervous.

The five men begin to push the Cadillac backward to the side of the highway behind the coal truck.

The bus jolts, the old men reach for their seats, bumping into each other.

"Hey, Rans, stop this slop bucket," says an old man,

his voice so deep McLain imagines an injured throat. "Let a body see what the hell's going on."

When Rans stops the bus again, McLain walks to the front. "Listen, I've got to get to Black Damp soon as possible. . . . My mother's dying."

"You don't *sound* like you're from around here, mister," says Rans, looking up at McLain as if he doesn't believe him.

"I've been away. Up North."

"I figured . . ."

"My brother lives around here, though, in Harmon. . . . I'd appreciate your not stopping unless you have to. . . ."

"Okay, mister, leave it to me, you're in good hands when you travel with Rans. Ain't that right, Mr. Satterfield?"

"That's right, Rans," said one of the old men behind McLain.

"Now, these old fellers here got all the time in the world," says Rans. "We dropping 'em off at Harmon for a little reunion of the disaster of nineteen and twenty-one."

"That was before my time," says McLain, trying to be friendly.

Returning to his seat, McLain looks at his watch. Five o'clock. The mountains, like Manhattan skyscrapers, make darkness come early.

"Truckston!" announces Rans. "Here she *comes* . . . There she *goes!*"

In the reek of bodies on the bus, McLain imagines his mother, her breath coming in tiny explosions, lying in the iron bed where his six brothers and five sisters were born —four dying in infancy or early childhood of diseases— where he was the last to be born, a few months after his father had suffocated a mile underground. After her funeral, he will sleep as he must have slept the first day of his life, and wake to gaze through veils of half-sleep upon the company town—as strange to him now as it must have been then.

"Somebody's playing with that snow-machine up yonder. Keeps shutting off and on." The old men think Rans is a card. McLain does not.

In the gray light, a coal truck passes, overloaded, a light skin of snow over the chunks of coal. Hairpin curves, smoke from cigars and rancid pipes, the old men's voices, fits of snow on the windows—McLain dozes.

Fall asleep, I might freeze to death. "Say driver, I wonder if you'd mind turning your heater on?"

"Elmo, is he making fun of me?"

"Can't never *tell* about a Yankee," a one-armed old man replies, goodnaturedly.

McLain wishes he could see the mountains the bus is crossing. He has gone back only in dreams and nightmares. The contrast—being physically in the mountains after eleven years— is a shock, producing nausea, inducing sleep. He slept flying across the continent from San Francisco. In fits of wakefulness between naps on the plane, he felt a drowsy eagerness to see again the mountain landscape that has haunted his dreams. He hates the way these people live, but he can not reject the mountains that helped to set their style. In his travels for ABC, he was always aware that whenever he moved toward or into mountains, or could simply *see* them from a distance, he began to unwind. But in the lowlands, in the cities, remembering the life he had escaped disgusted him. He had talked himself out of the assignment to cover the explosion of Consolidation Coal Company's Number 9 in

Farmington, West Virginia, in December last year, not expecting that the coverage would continue for days, giving him the exposure he needed to make CBS aware of him.

" 'Let's remember Pearl Harbor. . . .' " A hunchbacked old man startles his seat partner.

"Who's that singing?" asks the deep voice.

"It's a two-headed anniversary. 'And go on to vic-tor-ry. . . .' "

"But ours comes first. Twenty years ever before I give thought *one* to a Jap."

"Besides," says another old man, "it's December twenty-first, not seventh."

And three men are on their way to the moon. McLain shakes his head at the willful ignorance of a busload of old men.

The old men reminisce about the mine explosion in Harmon in 1921. McLain tries to remember hearing about it when he was growing up, but he has forgotten. Their voices are weaker than Rans's. Over the rattle and rumble of the bus, McLain catches fragments. The picture that takes shape is of ten old men, some crippled, some one-legged, some crook-backed, some blind, some afflicted with black lung, journeying to a reunion with other survivors of one of the earliest catastrophes in Appalachian coal-mining. McLain catches the names of those who perished: Grayden, Garland, Buck, Morgan, Frank, Woodrow, Kennis, Hop, Lonzie, Toney. These survivors had moved on to other minefields, perhaps a few to Black Oak before it became notorious for methane gas poisoning and its name was changed to Black Damp.

McLain wants to ask if they remember Tavilas Grybus, but he doesn't want to get drawn into the group. If the rest of the world had forgotten an event it once thought unforgettable, these old men would not have forgotten. Had his father survived the Black Oak explosion of 1931, perhaps he would be sitting among these old codgers, and McLain, living under his father's, not his mother's name, would be.... Where *would* he be? Working in the mines? McLain doesn't want to listen, yet he *does* want to listen, but he doesn't want to get drawn *in*.

"Now, I don't remember that feller there."

"I been trying to place him, but for the *life* of me. . . ."

The two old men in front of McLain are silent a while. Then the one-armed man leans across the aisle, holding to the seat in front of him with his only hand, and says, "Hey, mister!" A hunched old man turns around. "We been studying. What's *your* name?"

"Fred Stooksbury."

"Said 'Fred Stooksbury,' " says the one-armed man to his partner. "Well, I don't recall . . . ," he says to the hunched man.

"Don't you remember me? I'm the feller used to always go—" he does a rusty imitation of an old-time locomotive—"and we'd be way underground, and I'd yell, 'Watch it, boys, here comes the Cincinnati *ex*press!' and every time, some new feller'd forget and jump back, and we'd all laugh. Remember?"

"That's a good 'un. Bet *that* give us all a good laugh."

"Oh, yeah, it was a killer."

"You remember what he's talking about?" the one-armed man asks his friend.

"Seems like I ort to, but for the *life* of me . . . ."

'For the world's one breathing . . . .' The words bewilder McLain until he remembers the dream and grasps for the rest. *'. . . . may attain at last true time.' No, 'may attain*

at first *true time.*' "First" seemed so strange last night that now he had quite naturally said "last." After the party, celebrating the end of his first continued report over CBS television, the San Francisco State College riots, McLain tossed and turned until four A. M. Then, out of a half-waking dream came: "For the world's one breathing may attain at first true time." Deliberately, so he could remember the words, he forced himself awake. Then he slept until the telephone rang at seven, and his brother said, "Kenneth? This is Carl. You better come down here, Momma's almost gone." Like the old mountain folk, like his own mother—knowing, when the baby kicked violently in her belly, that its father was trapped in the mine —McLain had dreamed a premonition.

"Buckrock!" announces Rans. "Here she *comes.* . . . There she *goes.* . . ."

A short way along the valley, TRUCKS CROSSING shows up in the bus lights. The bus slows. Seeing gigantic logs, McLain remembers the days of the logging boom during the war. Bright lights flooding the bus through the front windows make him squint. Looking between the old men's heads across the aisle through the windows, Mc-Lain sees an official car parked on the wrong side of the highway, its lights on bright.

A smaller light bounces up to the driver's side of the bus. Rans slides back his window, letting in a spume of snow that curls like a scarf around his neck and fizzles out gently over the heads of the old men.

"That you, Rans?"

"What you doing with your badge on, Hutch?"

"You see anybody afoot?"

"Yeah. Several."

"One of them was probably Harl Abshire."

"Now *I'll* tell one!"

"He was *spotted*. Stold a Cadillac off somebody. Gas run dry on him in the middle of the highway, and he struck out a-walking it. Reverend Weaver recognized him, offered him a ride, and he lit out running, off into the trees."

"Man that busted out nine years ago, I can't feature him running still."

"We hoped he'd be on this bus."

"Well, if he was, it'd be for free, 'cause I ain't forgot."

"You talk just like the *rest* of 'em."

"And proud *of* it. Mind if I move on? I'm carrying a man that needs to be in Black Damp."

As the bus begins to roll, it occurs to McLain that they might this instant be injecting into his mother's veins the artificial blood of the corpse.

McLain touches a hole in the upholstery of his seat. His numb fingers feel the sharp point of paper tucked there. A love-note, intricately folded, such as he had passed in the white frame schoolhouse. "Dear Lamar, Where *were* you? Love, Tama." McLain refolds it, replaces it, and imagines Lamar reading it.

This morning, Ann and her two kids were among the thousands who watched the Apollo 8 blast-off. He had not had a chance to tell her not to come. Tonight, while the kids go to a movie, she will come to his motel. When the doorbell rings, David Stein will answer. McLain feels that missing his most important coverage for CBS is a disaster, but he suspects that missing his first rendezvous with Ann is, as his mother would say, "a blessing in disguise," for one day she will obtain her divorce, and McLain doesn't want to marry her kids.

"Ain't a jail built by man can hold Harl Abshire." With

his cane, the old man whacks the seat in front to stress his point.

"Let the other Abshires get word of this," said the deep-voiced man, "and won't all the deputies in these mountains be able to hold him."

"If they catch him," said a blind man.

You said it, brother, thinks McLain. *The word made flesh. Bigger than words, bigger than life. Even bigger than TV. The drowsy lid, the slack jaw, the snuff-streaked cracked lips, hands limp in lap, reason slack, the pores of the mind closed to foreign matter, wide open to fables. And why not? A hunger the tongue can taste and tell. The compulsion to tell it. Veils of tobacco smoke drifting inside, veils of snow drifting outside.* Beginning to *see* the fugitive now, via the telstar of his imagination, McLain sneers, for he has never heard of Harl Abshire and doesn't like to believe that new legends are born out of such sterile soil. He tries deliberately to see the astronauts, the earth receding at their backs, the moon looming larger, but he cannot get them in focus. When McLain wakes up in Black Damp, they will wake up circling the moon.

"This cold dropped sudden," says Rans. "They was *working* on this highway when I come through here this morning."

As the bus moves across the mountains at a hiker's pace toward Black Damp, McLain thinks of his mother as a skinny old hawk, moldering in her nest. She has never been beyond Harmon, twelve miles from Black Damp, nor wished to see beyond her view of slate dumps, collapsed coal tipples, and dirt slides from strip mining on the surrounding hills. McLain's constant motion and his parents' stasis are relative in time, he realizes, for his great-

great-grandfather McLain, an indentured servant, fled a Virginia plantation and lived with an Indian woman in a cave in these mountains—a fugitive for seventy years. The blood of the exterminated Indians still flows in McLain's dying mother. His father had spent half his life dreaming of escaping his native land, a country so small and obscure, McLain once spent an hour looking for it on the schoolhouse map. When he was twenty, his father fled Lithuania, following rumors of the American Dream, and, in a region the nation now regarded as a nightmare, found the quiet bliss of a hard work some men call slavery. And the second half of his life, his father had burrowed deeper and deeper into black gold. Had Tavilas Grybus stayed in Lithuania, McLain would be living now in a country Russia had swallowed. The idea of trying to persuade his mother to see these speculative ironies makes him smile. For his mother called his own escape from Black Damp an unforgivable crime against her and his father. Though he doesn't believe in the crime any more, he is still trying to shake off the guilt. But the force that draws his thoughts if not his body back, no matter how many miles of land and culture he puts between Black Damp and himself, is not just guilt. It is a nostalgia that mocks all his achievements and ambitions, for he feels no nostalgia for the scenes of his gradual escape and ascent— Lexington, Huntington, Pittsburgh.

The bus slides into a curve. The snow is packing and freezing.

"Rans, stop and ask that man does he know anything about Harl."

"You ain't no curiouser than *I* am, but I got a man on here trying to get to his dyin' mother. Schedule has to be met—that's all!"

Turning his head, pressing his cheek against the cold pane, McLain glimpses a man bent over against the snow, trudging up the mountain.

"She was a Hobbs before she married old Abshire," says the man with the injured voice, and most of the others, catching the name, turn around, or lean across the aisle. "Drug him off that hillside rock-farm to breathe coaldust. Them days you worked by candlelight till midnight . . . . you drug in and fell like a tree cut down on the bed—barely miss your ten-year-old boy as he got up to take your place." The sudden realization that the old man is performing for *his* benefit, startles McLain and he feels shy. "Well, one day Harl says to Mr. Keathley, 'Today, I've turned fourteen and I reckon hit's bout time I *re*tired.' After that he never went *inside* a mine, 'cept to plant that dynamite they hired him to set off in May of nineteen and fifty-nine. Took the money them union boys gave 'im and bought coal that he dumped on every unemployed porch in town. That year when the snow was worse than it is now."

"Didn't folks claim it was the worst snow of the century?"

A while later, McLain hears a car pass at high speed, sees it take a steep curve in front of the bus as Rans mashes on his horn with a flourish. "That's okay, neighbor, we'll be along to pick up the pieces d'reckly."

"Shoot," says the blind man, "I bet my ass that was Harl—stold him another Cadillac."

McLain tries to stay awake, straining to listen to the old men. Though they talk of different things their voices meld in a harmonious drone.

"My boy just come back from *De*troit. Not a lick of work *no*where."

"Wick Thompson brung his whole family back from Chicago last week. Come a strike, he said he'd rather starve around home."

McLain remembers the riots in Cleveland last August, the strange sight of looters moving slowly down the sidewalk, as if attracted by a magnet, to a store directly in front of Albert's TV cameras, McLain cautiously moving closer, holding the mike to pick up the voices and the noises of merchandise being wrenched from neat displays.

Suddenly, the sound of a locomotive. Everybody turns and looks at the old man. He croaks: "Watch it, boys, here comes the Cincinnati *ex*press!" But nobody responds with recognition to the old horse play routine.

Embarrassed, McLain gazes out the window. Snow, tons of it, falling. Still, as two centuries ago when white man and red man huddled together in the caves one can still see, alongside the auger holes.

"Get ready to cuss, mister, when we hit Hightown," says Rans, his voice sounding different when he speaks to McLain.

"How come?" McLain feels silly, yelling conversationally over the heads of the old men as some turn to look at him.

"Strike. Streets full of folks milling around. Move? Hell, they wouldn't move for a coal truck coming a hundred miles an hour. Poke along from curb to curb like they got forever."

The bus enters Hightown just as a train's caboose clears a crossing.

"Look at that!" says Rans. A plastic Santa Claus hangs from a street light over the main intersection. "Thanksgiving dishes still in the sink and here it is Christmas!"

Looped from pole to pole, other decorations hang along the street.

"Well, they got him!" says Rans. McLain recognizes the mountain tone of satisfaction that the inevitable has come to pass.

The old men rise to peer through the glass the wipers have smeared. McLain sees groups of people up ahead— two bunches along the right curb, another strung out from them like an arm, reaching toward the railroad track that crosses the busiest street in the middle of town.

At the edge of the crowd by the curb, Rans stops the bus. "I reckon I damn well have to get out and look, too, mister."

"Listen, I've paid my fare to get to Black Damp."

"Hell," says Rans, getting out, "I'm from around here myself."

Standing in the doorway of the empty bus, reluctant to intrude, hoping Rans will remain aware of him and feel impelled to resume the journey shortly, McLain looks down upon the three separate groups, people in each distracted by activities in the others.

Nearest the bus, people hover around a wounded policeman. Others squat in two ragged rows, examining a trail of blood that leads to the railroad crossing. The policeman's cap lies crown down in the gutter, snow rising in the bowl of it as slush drips from the soles of his shoes.

A larger crowd huddles around a pregnant woman who stands on the curb hugging her son's face against her belly. Around her feet in the gutter lie dented cans, labels smeared, a squashed loaf of bread, liver in plastic wrap. An old man wearing a miner's helmet holds a can of pork and beans, and a young woman keeps brushing snow off a bag of corn meal. The pregnant woman's son holds a carton of eggs, the yolk of a broken one dribbling onto the toe of his shoe. The rest of her groceries, too mangled to pick up, lie around her feet.

". . . coming out of the A & P," she is saying, catching her breath after each word to suppress hysteria, "when he come right at me and kissed me smack in the mouth."

"I *saw* it," says the old man in the miner's helmet. "He stepped right up to her, and her with a bag of groceries in one arm, holding the boy's hand with the other, and he looked to me he had tears in his eyes before he kissed her all of a sudden."

"I never knowed a Abshire to shed tear." McLain can't see who spoke.

"Then what?" a girl asks the pregnant woman.

"I dropped my groceries and he bent to pick 'em up, then Sherman come over and said something to him, and Harl shot him and commenced to run in the street and Sheriff Clevenger come out of the café shooting at him and hit him and he kept staggering toward the tracks and jumped on the caboose of the train."

A tubercular-looking man muscles into the inner circle of the crowd and looks at the woman, the boy, and the groceries. "What happened here?"

"I saw it happen," said the old man, holding the can of beans in both hands, peering from under the helmet as if from under a rock.

"Let *her* tell it."

"I was just coming out of the A & P and he comes right up to me and kisses me on the mouth."

"And it was Harl Abshire?"

"Sure as the world *was*."

"*Then* what?"

"Well, I drop my groceries on the sidewalk."

"He hurt you?"

"No, it was just that it *floored* the fool out of me."

"What did he say?"

"Nothing. Tried to catch my groceries before the poke burst and it all spilled out, him clutching that broken poke against his belly, half-squatted."

"And then what?"

"And then Sherman come up to us and he says, 'Harl, they alooking for you.' Stooped over to him, you know, with his hands on his knees—me in the middle."

The boy twists his face, red from the cold and his mother's grasping affection, and looks up at her.

"What'd Harl *say?*" asks the tubercular man.

"Not a word, he just let the poke slip and reaches over like reaching across the table for a biscuit and takes Sherman's pistol out of his holster and shoots him."

Powder burns had blackened her hands that press the boy's shoulder toward the cradle of her hips. *When her hands thaw*, thinks McLain, *they'll hurt.*

"Maybe he didn't hear what it was Sherman said."

"Likely he didn't." McLain loves the way her mouth moves.

"How come him to kiss you, lady?"

"If they catch him, I'd like to ask him that one myself. And why he let you damned men hire him to blow up that tipple in fifty-nine and get his ass throwed in Harmon jail—and where he's been since he busted out nine years ago."

"You knowed him before?"

"Before he kissed me?"

"Hell, man," says a grocery clerk who has run out into the cold coatless, "her and Harl was sweethearts back yonder."

"You looking for trouble?" She doesn't even look at the man. McLain shivers.

"Don't ever' man along Red Bird Creek know it?"

"Yeah, and now ever' man in Hightown'll know it—my husband to boot."

"*Then* what did Harl do?" asks the tubercular man.

"Say, who the hell *are* you, anyway? Some deputy?"

"No, ma'am. I'm from just up the pike a ways."

"Well, he jumps that freight that was passing through."

Coal gondolas. Blood and snow and slag and the smell of gunpowder and the taste of a woman's mouth. McLain wants to kiss her himself, go home with her, make love to her, inhaling the fumes of coal burning in the grate.

Her eyes rove erratically over the faces around her, but though McLain is elevated in the stairwell of the bus, they don't fall on *his* face. *All that's missing*, he thinks, *is a television camera*. He knows that if he were in possession of a mike, he would be in possession of the scene, and thus of her. And he would not be invisible to her as he was now, but the realest person in Hightown.

Hoping to persuade Rans to move on, McLain steps down, into a vacant place left by a man the sheriff has sent away on an errand. As the sheriff turns back to the wounded policeman, McLain bends over and watches the victim's eyes open.

"I just said to him, 'Harl, they alooking for you," says Sherman. "We used to deer hunt together when we's boys. But I reckon he didn't see my face for my cap. I didn't mean him no harm in this world, Sheriff."

Momentarily, Sheriff Clevenger's shoulder eclipses

Sherman's face, then moves again, revealing Sherman's
eyes where the light glows faintly, then goes out.

The Sheriff staggers backward as he gets up, scuffing
blood into the snow. Looking into McLain's eyes, he says,
"Well, maybe *this*'ll satisfy 'em awhile." The intimacy in
his voice makes McLain blink, awkwardly. "Who are *you*,
mister?"

"Kenneth McLain, trying to get to Black Damp."

"To who?" The Sheriff's knees are wet.

"My mother may be dead by now."

Sheriff Clevenger looks at McLain blankly, then turns
away.

Three men stare at McLain. Their eyes glance down,
then up, then stare. Looking down, he steps backward out
of the blood.

"*Then* what happened?" someone asks the woman.

McLain moves closer to the curb.

"He kissed me. Leaned over my grocery bag and kissed
me right on the lips."

"Drunk, I bet."

"Tasted like Pabst Blue Ribbon." The pregnant woman smiles for the first time.

Rans is climbing back into the bus. Men, women, and
children crowd on behind him with such violent and common impulse that he is lifted up the last step and hurled
into his seat. The door shuts McLain out. He scuttles
around the front of the slowly moving bus to the driver's
window, using his cold knuckles to knock on the glass.

Rans looks down at McLain. "One man's got to get
off!"

The doors open, a boy steps down, and McLain shoves
himself up into the stairwell, crams himself between two
young men in miner's clothes. The single lamp on their

helmets and the grime on their faces subdue their eyes as they look into his.

The bus jolts over the railroad tracks. Through nearly opaque panes in the door, McLain sees the woman on the curb, hugging her child, telling it again. Her lips signify, "I was coming out of the A & P . . . ," but McLain can't hear her voice.

"He'll jump off in the woods before the next crossing." As much certainty vibrated in Rans's voice going out the west side of town as when he had said, "Well, they got him," coming in on the east side.

The bus is packed now with people who want to catch up with Harl Abshire, but who don't want the Sheriff to capture him. They have given seats to the crippled among the old men, and the blind man sits in the front seat above where McLain stands in the stairwell.

"If he was ever going with her, *I* never heard tell of it."

"Fact I never heard of her at all." This old man leans forward from the seat behind the blind man. "Some Damrons up Red Bird Creek, but no Rhetha *I* know of."

"Well, *now* you do," said a man in overalls, who was not in the group going to Harmon for the reunion of the survivors of the 1921 explosion.

"A boy half-grown and another simmering on the back of the stove."

"Reckon who's the father of the first—the one that looks to be *nine* years old?" A woman in a coat the style of the Thirties, probably donated through the Red Cross after last spring's flood, draws the attention of the men seated near her and others standing over her, and she is pleased.

Though the incident was simple enough in naked outline, no tongue, not even his mother's, could tell lucidly enough what the boy's blue eyes had seen.

The bus is a packed hive of talk, heat, smoke, stale breath. Dizzy, swaying on his feet, unable to doze. Mc-Lain picks out phrases and snatches of talk.

"More traffic than normal, and the weather worse than usual."

"Roaming around, hoping to get a glimpse of The Fugitive. Hey, that one still on TV?"

"Not if you live in the valley, but up on Pine Mountain, my sister gets it."

"After nine years, ain't nobody can tell it the way it happened."

"Well, say you had the facts? What would you do with them?"

"File 'em away, I reckon."

"Give me a good story *any* day."

Reflected on the windshield, Rans's face glows green and red, his eyes catching sparks of light from the dash panel. As the bus moves up and down mountainsides, the wipers flicker like a camera shutter, and the road winds up on the spool of the wheels like television tape, developed differently by each person on the bus, all of them feeling the same rhythm coming up through the rubber of the tires into the soles of their feet as they stand, through the cushions into their butts where they sit. Harl's eyes are the lens of a TV camera, thinks McLain, recording at high speed, mindlessly, as he runs, scenes Mc-Lain and other witnesses reach moments later.

"Harl sent the money in secret some way and they had the monument put up for his momma and daddy."

"Harl was a feller always liked a body to be remembered."

"*Was?* Shut up that *was.* Let Sheriff Abshire—I mean, Clevenger—say *was,* if he can."

"Say, mister," asks one of the old men, looking down into the stairwell, "ain't I seen you somewheres before?"

"Maybe."

"You might not *sound* like you're from around here, but your face ain't a stranger."

Imagining the old man sitting in front of his television, saying to his wife, "I like that young feller's face," delights McLain. But the old man's eyes will dim out one evening soon, as McLain stands in hot sunlight in Jerusalem in front of a café a terrorist's bomb has blown to splinters and sand.

When he became an announcer for the television station in Huntington, he imagined his mother sitting alone in the house, her only neighbors the other two widows allowed to live in the defunct company town, watching him on the news. When he went on to Pittsburgh as a newscaster and later to New York City on a local station, knowing that she couldn't pick him up always depressed him. But when he had finally got a position with ABC last February, he imagined his mother watching all the news shows, hoping to catch a glimpse of him, proud of her son when he reported about Murf the Surf from Miami, Robert Kennedy's campaign from California, the race riot from Cleveland, the eruption of a dead volcano from Costa Rica, the murder of Ramon Navarro from Hollywood, Jackie's wedding from Greece, the peace talks from Paris. And as she watched man circle the moon, he had hoped to explain it all to her from Cape Kennedy. But this morning Carl had told him on the telephone that for the past year his mother had lived alone in Black

Damp, and, the other two widows having died, the electricity from Harmon had been cut off.

There is a chance the bus will get him to Black Damp before she dies, and that chance now seems as important to him as the one her dying has denied him. For a man has to get exposure. Look at Dan Rather. He happened to be in Dallas when Kennedy was shot. For days, the nation saw and heard his reports. A few months later, he was reporting from the White House lawn. McLain has been fighting a long time for a chance like that. Following McCarthy and then Kennedy, he watched the sustained coverage of Martin Luther King's assassination, of the student riots at the Sorbonne, of the assassination of Robert Kennedy, of the launching of Apollo 7 with the feeling of having missed some great opportunities for exposure. His feature on the girl who shot Warhol was never used, although the one he did on wall paintings in Harlem streets was shown. His sustained reports from Resurrection City in Washington resulted in an offer from CBS. For weeks he had been covering the student riots at San Francisco State—he looks at his watch—and right at this moment, David Stein is taking his place at Cape Kennedy. It is six o'clock, and he hears a voice, clearly: "This is the CBS Evening News, with Harry Reasoner in New York . . . Dan Rather in Washington . . . Roger Mudd in San Francisco . . . Mike Wallace in Paris . . . Eric Sevareid in New York . . . Kenneth McLain at Cape Kennedy . . . and Walter Cronkite at Cape Kennedy." Now at this "great moment in history"—he hears the voice of Walter Cronkite—McLain's mother is dying and David Stein takes his place. He hates himself for blaming his mother. But her forgiveness for the past and her blessing for the future will be almost enough to make up for the loss.

The bus stops again. The shuddering idle of the old World War II military bus makes McLain feel simultaneously his mother's and Harl's labored breathing, and his own becomes fitful. Dreading another delay, McLain looks between two heads out the front window. The bus lights make the back of a car stand out vividly, though the snow is an undulating curtain. The Sheriff's car, leading the caravan, is parked in the road up the hill, its lights shining on coal gondolas that block the highway at a crossing. They are searching the train and the surrounding woods. As McLain stares, trying to get the total picture and make sense of it, the snow stops.

"I'm getting off here, Rans. See my cousin's Chevvie."

"Damned if it ain't Deer Creek crossing! Believe I'll walk it from here. He just might cut up 78 to Raby. I know that holler like I know my own shoes."

When Rans opens the door, a wall of cold air presses against McLain's back and seeps in among the packed bodies, dissipating the hot vapor of breath and body heat that has made him sweat.

"Or he might take a notion to cut south to Breezy," says an old woman wearing an army overcoat. "Come on, Cecil." A fat man in his late thirties takes her hand, stumbles off the bus behind her, drooling, "Snow's stop, snow's stop. . . ."

As others follow, McLain flings himself into one of the empty seats by a window. Car lights come toward the bus. McLain stands again and sees through the front window that the coal train has moved on. The bus begins to roll. Near the crossing, McLain sees cars in front turn off, north and south onto 78, into black wilderness.

"More highway patrol boys toward Harmon," says an old man, sizing up the situation.

A few cars continue west toward Harmon and Black Damp. At the crossing, more people get off the bus. Now, only McLain and the maimed old men and a few others remain. He returns to his original seat. His small suitcase has served as a footstool for muddy shoes.

McLain notices one old man who has not yet spoken, and when others speak to him, he just sits there, like a tongue-tied child. But, somehow his silence gives force and authority to what the others say. With a fellow-feeling for the old man, because McLain himself is silent, McLain glances at him now and then, wanting to hear, if he *does* speak.

Out there, beyond the frosted glass, are the woods. Puny woods since the logging days and after the fires each year. McLain sees only snowbanks that seem to foam against the bus. Above them, darkness. But he imagines trees, ground, pits under the snow that can wrench an ankle as suddenly as a sneeze stops the heart. And Harl is running, gun in hand, steely air rasping his throat, his heart shuddering through his stomach, his legs, his pounding feet, packing down snow. Blood has congealed around the wound, the brass bullet stinging like a wasp. Or has he fallen against the dull-blade edge of a cold rock? Sheriff Clevenger would be glad to see glistening blood.

Watching the headlights of oncoming cars—many one-eyed—approach from far up the highway and pass the bus makes McLain sleepy.

Waking, he feels a hip against his own. "Harl? That you?"

"You all hear that?" The high voice sounds electronically augmented, like a kid's in a rock band. The hip is

sharp, an old man's. "Feller thinks I'm Harl Abshire."
Cackles clatter in the dark, sharp air. For a moment, Mc-
Lain thinks it is the silent man. "Got a cigar you'll turn
loose of for a nickel?"

"Sorry, I don't smoke."

"I need me a good old Red Dot," he says, getting up.
Rans shifts gears and the one-armed old man lunges
back to his seat in front of the silent man.

Nine years since Harl broke out of Harmon jail,
thinks McLain. *What's he been doing all that time?
HONEST CITIZEN OF PLEASANTVILLE, OHIO
UNMASKED AS FUGITIVE. The wife and kids will
receive word of his flight. Disillusionment. But not hiding in the hills all that time, surely. Reel nine, butchered
by forty years' mishandling in the nation's projection
booths.* McLain turns to look out the window, sees only
his own dull eyes on the pane against the dark. *Then
suddenly out of nowhere (think of the millions of things
that come out of nowhere—most overpopulated place
known to man) an out-of-state mauve Cadillac, abandoned in the middle of Highway 80 outside Truckston,
straddling the line, gas tank bone dry. Warm as toast inside, the wipers waving goodbye to Harl, hello to Rans
and passengers, as the lights dim and blink and implode.
Like the heart's last voltage, seen in the eyes. Survivor's
reunion. Mythmaker's reunion. Rake their balls as they
talk—radiant heat. Eat, smoke, wipe, spit, fart, rake balls,
lift butt and shift, pat belly, belch—embellishments on the
evolving figure of the fugitive that bestrides the snow-
spread landscape like a figure on a cave wall. The darkness, the cigar, pipe, and cigarette smoke obscure the eyes.
Blind old Homers. The ruby lights from the dash, the
sweeping lights of passing cars, show only shadowed sock-*

ets. Some are eyeless, some lack eyeballs though not the inner light, but all are black hollows in the moving dark of the bus. Blind old Homers. Bards. . . . Rhetha's eyes as Harl kissed her. . . . And did my mother's eyes close forever in that moment? For the world's one breathing may attain at first true time.

Snow again on the windshield, spitting, trying to stick, wind-whipped.

McLain sleeps in the bed where he used to sleep with three brothers and sisters and his mother, and wakes a few moments later, still on the Red Bird bus. "We to Harmon yet?"

"Not yet." Unable to tell who spoke, McLain wonders if it was the silent man.

"White Station!" announces Rans. "Here she *comes* . . . There she *goes!*"

McLain overhears the old man with the hunched back say to his seatmate, "Don't it seem like you ort to *know* that face?"

As the old man answers, "Well, it being so dark in here . . ." McLain imagines him leaning across the aisle, staring at his face.

"What you want to bet this turns out the worst snow of the century?" asks another old man.

Did something blossom in Harl Abshire, then fall to seed and fester, McLain wonders, until he had to act? Impulse struck him. In his bed at night beside a respectable, ignorant wife . . . on the toilet in the morning . . . on the road to work in some factory—where? In Indianapolis, Chicago, Detroit, Baltimore? Or some small town? And he had stolen a Cadillac and simply driven in the general direction of his dreams, run out of gas, and started hiking it, as in the old days. Until he came to

Hightown. As strange to him now as Black Damp will be to McLain. He imagines Harl looking for Rhetha at her old house, finding sunken foundations and weeds, or a strange family, or a landslide from strip-mining higher up on the mountain. He searches. Suddenly, he sees her standing on a curb in front of the brutally new A & P, hugging groceries, holding her son's hand, about to step off against the traffic.

What did her boy see? Something to compete with events on television? A happening? A love-in? Who sponsored this Candid Camera setup, this comic situation that backfired? One day, the boy will go over the chronology of his life, and the possibility may occur to him that the man who kissed his mother, then shot a policeman with his own gun, and leapt onto a train passing through town, was his own father. To be given an opportunity to reinterpret radically all one's life up to a certain moment— an exhilarating sense of rebirth? Or the precipitation of a slow dying? *That boy. That boy.* To be envied or pitied?

McLain feels now the loss of his own children. He has lost touch with the girl he met and married in Lexington and who divorced him in Huntington. From the girl he married and divorced in Pittsburgh, he gets only a Christmas card each year, with a group picture of her and the boy and the girl McLain sometimes longs to see in the flesh. His father loved the mines. Well, McLain likes his freewheeling life in New York, always on the move.

In the dark bus, where he sees nothing inside or outside, McLain sees fields full of sunken, rusted machinery, trash dumps, slag heaps, auger holes, coal smoke pouring out of chimneys, wrecked cars in dry creek beds, swinging bridges, mineshafts, junk put to bizarre uses in yards, burnt hillsides, strip and pit mines. When it was still daylight, he saw below him, then lost it, then saw it again above him, a clearing for the expressway that Carl said would wipe out Black Damp by next summer and link the mountains with the U. S. highway.

Where Indians once scalped pioneers of his blood in the forgotten past, merchants in the near future will bloodlessly scalp the tourists who will come to see the driftmouth of the mine where Tavilas Grybus was trapped in 1931. The Chamber of Commerce in nearby Harmon will resurrect that story, which, even as far as Asia, had lived in the headlines for a week. In summer, the log cabins in the hills will be air-conditioned, in winter boarded up. This region that had overslept, yawning in the face of the twentieth century, will finally awaken from the Age of Coal and start to dress for the Age of Space. On the fringe, still, ghostlike denim figures blink at the strange transformation. But the denim too is in the final fadeout. The dead clichés will be resurrected in new shapes and fabrics, and CBS will present them live. Black Damp died five years before McLain fled from it, and now they will bury the decomposed corpse under a lava flow of asphalt. McLain knows that he has never made the break. Now tractors and bulldozers are doing *for* him what he has been unable to do for himself.

Harl hurls himself through the woods, leaving a ragged trail of blood on the snow. *Don't kill him, just catch him. Or let him flag the bus and ride out of Sheriff Clevenger's reach, but move—get me there, Rans. . . .* McLain realizes that the life of the legend will be briefer than his own life, because when these blind Homers die, the habit of nonutilitarian speech will vanish from the earth. So

Harl may die tonight, and his story some day after to-morrow, but now, as he runs, he is free—in the lives, the racing imaginations of his witnesses—no past, no future, only the instant. McLain shuts his eyes wearily and hopes to sleep again.

He wakes to see the last of the old men step down in Harmon on a corner he doesn't recognize. They hobble blindly among coal tipples, a single yellow bulb dangling from each. He tries to make out the silent old man, but the dark figures coalesce into a stiff, almost immobile frieze, the silent, the blind, the one-armed, the one-legged, the hunchbacked, indistinguishable from each other.

"Black Damp coming *up!*" announces Rans.

His father's bones never saw the light of day. But Mc-Lain did. And he and his mother and brothers and sisters stayed in Black Damp. The owner permitted them to live on in the town, even after the last of her sons left the mines to go to the war or to the defense plants or to the hospital with "black damp," and the mines themselves were sealed. McLain, light and bones, will flee for the last time, and his mother, with his father, and some of his brothers and sisters, will remain.

McLain often sat on the porch with his mother, lis-tening to her tell how much his father loved his life, though he saw daylight only on Sundays and then was "in a fit" to know what to do with himself. "He's bur-ied right where he lived. He never complained when he was alive, and you can bet your stars he ain't complain-ing now." McLain would look up at the driftmouth, but his imagination could never corroborate her testimony. "The mines'll come back. Just you wait and see." Afraid they might, McLain had not waited to see, he had gradu-ated from high school, knowing that that was the first step out of the mountains. As he grew up, he watched his brothers and sisters leave Black Damp, seldom returning, except for Carl, who taught science in Harmon High. And finally, when he was twenty, having been an announcer at the Harmon radio station for two years, McLain moved to Lexington and took his mother's family name. When he went back to see her at Christmas, she locked the door. But on her deathbed, the bed in which he was born, she will forgive him, release him.

He conjures up the three-room frame house with the small front porch, living room, bedroom, kitchen, the small back porch, the outhouse. Sitting in the television truck last summer during the Chicago police riots, he imagined her working in her garden of pole beans, to-matoes, cucumbers, morning glories climbing the front porch, the back porch, the outhouse, wearing an old-timey sunbonnet that was her mother's. Every spring, the Black Fork of the Pine River flooded the house, and after the water receded, she dragged all the furniture into the yard. Somehow the back streets of Saigon reminded him of the smell of the house in Black Damp, always rank with the odor of floods—one for each year of his past—the smell of fear for each year of his future. And in the fall, the suffocating, acrid smoke of brush fires mingled with the stench of floods and of smoldering slag heaps in the cracks and crevices of the house, in the mat-tresses dried in the sun, in his clothes, most of them do-nated after the flood of the year before. As he drifts into sleep again, McLain imagines the slag heaps among which he was born, and rains washing tons of mud down against his mother's white, soot-stained house, and rocks rolling down the denuded hills, hitting the roof. Like the people who lived on the slopes of active volcanoes, she felt at home, and all the places McLain had "covered" were alien.

Someone is pulling at him, he feels like a child, awakened in the night, shoved toward a cold doorway, who must run on numb feet, knees wobbly, to escape fire. Over his shoulder, he sees Rans, getting behind the steering wheel, revving the motor. Looking back into the cave of the bus, McLain sees that the seats are empty—except for the long one at the back, where a man sits, and as McLain stares at him, trying to see his face in the dark, the man slowly, very slowly, keels over. The man is Harl, and McLain decides that he is dreaming and can let himself fall the same way out of the stairwell of the bus into soft snow without hurting himself. He falls, it feels good to let go, he hits the ground, it hurts.

Snow melting in his mouth revives him. Exhaust fumes make him retch, sting his eyes. Veils of snowfall drift over red lights on the rear of the bus as they fade.

Pain, colors ringing in one eye, McLain stands. His eyes on the lamplight in the window of his mother's house, he walks over a white, uneven landscape. The barking of a dog becomes louder, faster, more vicious. As he walks toward the light, dragging his suitcase through the snow, his feet sinking almost to his knees, he is afraid, with each step, each labored breath, the lamp will go out.

The Shadow Knows

*A*LVIN stood at the open window in the kitchen, about to take the last bite of his peanut butter and banana sandwich. Uncle Bud sat on his parked Western Flyer, his Daisy air rifle cradled in his arms, looking up into the limbs and leaves of the oak tree that was stuffed with plaster where the trunk had rotted. Some of the starlings in the covey that circled the house would light on the telephone wires, a few would settle in the tree. Uncle Bud had on his gray Sunday suit, the right trouser leg rolled above the greasy chain, and a blue, man's hat. Ready to go.

The afternoon breeze cooled Alvin coming in, but at his back the wood stove was hot. Coming from the bathroom, Momma passed through the kitchen in her frayed mauve slip, on her way to the bedroom, where Gran'maw dropped hairpins onto the brass tray. "I thought I told you to stay out of that peanut butter. I've got a big supper simmering for when we get back, and that peanut butter'll just spoil it." He smelled the turnip greens bubbling behind him. Beyond Uncle Bud's shoulder, the railroad track curved out of the woods by the creek and passed between some houses, the semaphore blinking red, white sheets rippling on a line in the yard below the red clay bank. Alvin wanted to feel the cool, trembling rail under his ear, and listen.

Crossing the kitchen, he looked out the other window. Down the slope, the WPA ditch cut through the jungle, cleared once for new houses, then let run wild again when the Japs bombed Pearl Harbor. Alvin stepped through the window, the sill close to the ground, and went along the hedge toward the coal house. On the sunken piece of ground where the outhouse once stood, the speckled hens had settled snugly into the soft loam. He liked to be in under the ceiling of leaves and berries, the long low limbs of the hedge tree like rafters. The strong smell—chickens, yard, tree, coal house—made a zone of secrecy. Stepping over the sill into the coal house, he saw his Gran'paw astride a mule, pulling the red circus wagon down the alley, years before Alvin was born. Now it was full of coal and the kind of stuff that other people stored in attics. And behind the cream-yellow baby bed, streaked with coal dust, the holster lay under the World War I German helmet. They had hidden it in the back of the radio that had burned out a few years ago, and he had found it again. "You'll wear it out, or lose it, playing." Lifting the cool helmet with one hand, he grasped the soft leather with the other. He thrust his hand into it and smelled it.

Memorial Day. A wind stirring the birches among the white marble, the sun sinking in the chill air, the keen smell of flowers at his feet. They had taken him last year, and he had known that the piece of marble the size of a loaf of bread, initialed, and the shriveled, rank smelling stems thrown onto the next grave to make room in the jar for the fresh flowers had nothing to do with Gran'paw. It was all in the empty holster, the scent of the leather. If it wasn't for Memorial Day, he could wear it down to the ditch, and stand around outside the sewer pipe with Baby Jean. He slipped the holster down into the leg of his corduroy knickers and stepped down to the

ground again. The chickens hummed contentedly behind him, and Uncle Bud shot into the oak tree, flushing
seven starlings, dropping one.

Her glass pearls swinging from her neck, almost touching the sill, Momma leaned out the window. "Alvin!
Don't you dare set foot outside this yard. We'll be ready
to roll in exactly twenty minutes." When she closed the
window, Alvin felt the chill in the air. Twenty minutes!
Gran'maw, tasting the butter beans, must have streaked
the front of her dress.

He backed toward the coal house as Uncle Bud bent
to pick up the starling. Slipping along the side, ducking
under the hedge-berry tree, Alvin ran down the alley
toward the jungle. His feet slapped hard on the macadam,
but he felt as though he flew. He squatted at the edge
of the jungle and crawled through the weeds, briars, and
honeysuckle vines and slunk between the little trees to
the ditch. From the black hole of the sewer to the street,
it was empty. He wriggled among the vines to the street,
hoping to find Baby Jean on his front steps, reading the
funnies. "I can't, Baby Jean. It belonged to my gran'paw
when he was a night watchman. He wouldn't like nobody
but me to wear it." That was one thing he would never
let Baby Jean talk or threaten him into doing.

But everybody on Baby Jean's street had gone in.
Through the dining room window, Alvin saw him at the
supper table with his whole family, wolfing a chicken leg.
When his nose dripped the way gravy now drooled from
his chin, Baby Jean always added another snail track to
the back of his Lone Ranger glove.

Passing Baby Jean's wagon at the edge of the yard,
Alvin saw his own Dick Tracy automatic. A few days
after Christmas, he had found it under Baby Jean's front

steps, and when he said it was his, Baby Jean tackled him and pinned his arms to the ground. Everytime he got close to him, Baby Jean smelled like he had lost a race to the bathroom. Picking the automatic up out of the sandy bed of the wagon, Alvin swore that one day he would figure out a way to really fix old Baby Jean's trolley.

The short cut he had taken through the jungle forced him to cross the ditch. Squatting to jump off the edge, Alvin saw Yoyo biting burrs out of his long collie hair, one leg cocked up so he could get at them. He looked up, saw Alvin, started toward him, pausing to lap at a brown puddle in the curved center of the ditch. Alvin listened to the hedge-berry trees along the ditch shudder in the wind, then he jumped. The soles of his feet stung, and Yoyo almost knocked him down, rubbing his head against Alvin's still bent knees.

Alvin looped his belt through the holster, then thrust the Dick Tracy automatic into it and liked the heavy lay of it on his leg. Leaning against the rock wall of the rain ditch, he gazed into the black mouth of the sewer pipe that wound underground to Sandy Hook Creek. He twirled the broken-handled automatic, trying to do like Baby Jean, but dropped it, as he nearly always did. "Shoot fire!" He kept twirling it and dropping it, Yoyo watching, sitting in front of the sewer pipe. The sun had gone in, and under the gray sky the pistol clattered when it struck the rock bottom of the ditch. Yoyo sat, waited, panted, his tongue softly throbbing.

Through the limbs of a sycamore, Alvin looked at his gran'maw's house. On the slope, it was bone white. "There'll be blue birds over the white cliffs of Dover." Until the lights came on again all over the world and his

Daddy walked into the living room with his duffle bag over his shoulder, they were going to live in the house Gran'paw built with his own hands. Last month Uncle Bud blew out eighteen candles on a white coconut cake, and if he had to go to war, Alvin hoped he would let him take care of the Western Flyer. Before his feet could reach the pedals though, Uncle Bud would have to let down the seat. Beside the yellow fire plug, Momma's white De Soto coupe was parked. Alvin imagined the smell of the prickly seat, the sun pouring through the windshield.

It was like the warm morning sun on his mackinaw in the ditch the time just before Easter when he told Baby Jean about the gun he was going to get to go in the holster. "Let's us play Gang Busters, Baby Jean," he had said.

"Gang Buster's nothin to play when I got on my new Lone Ranger outfit!" He slapped his fancy holster. Then he looked hard at Alvin. "Tell you what. You let me wear your gran'paw's holster and I'll play Gang Busters with you."

Alvin had stepped back, shuddered when a sharp rock in the wall jabbed his spine. His cold hand grasping the soft leather, he shook his head, the inside corners of his eyes prickling.

"I ain't gonna play nothin then. I just wanted to try *on* the rotten thing. You don't even have no gun for it."

Alvin didn't remind Baby Jean of what happened to his Dick Tracy automatic. "I don't care about that. One of these days I'm gonna get me a real gun for it and go off lookin for the lowlife rat that kilt my gran'paw when his back was turned."

"Done *what!*" His eyes and mouth open wide, Baby Jean had stepped sideways, back and forth a couple of times.

He had always supposed Baby Jean would laugh if he told him. Alvin had begged to hear it over and over ever since he was four, and they had told him so many times that he could tell it himself more easily than Mother Goose rhymes. It used to be a good way to get his whole family laughing. He had stopped telling anybody. Just thought about growing up, going out, looking, even if he had to hunt over every foot of Knoxville. But Baby Jean had kept on wanting to know.

"Well, my gran'paw used to own a whole lot of lumber, but when the depression come, he lost ever stick of it, and it come to where all he could do was hire out as a night watchman in another lumber yard or starve." Alvin had had to look at the bug-black entrance to the sewer pipe to keep from watching Baby Jean's nose run green. "He had him a gun he carried in this here same holster when he'd walk around the lumber yard at night, cocked to kill anybody that'ud try to steal any lumber. So what happened—one mornin, he was washin up in the bathroom of the lumber yard an had his gun layin on the toilet seat when in come this mean ol' man that was mad at him cause he was after his job an that man took up my gran'paw's gun an fore he knew what was comin off, shot him in the back with it. An he's still runnin loose sommers."

"I don't believe a word *of* it," said Baby Jean, the first time he had ever sounded jealous of Alvin. He had a two storey house, a room of his own, all kinds of broken toys flooding the floor, a rocking horse in the corner that he'd rocked to death, two brothers and a big sister, even though they couldn't stand him around, and a collie that would rather follow Alvin.

Thinking of Baby Jean made Alvin so angry, he picked up a rock and threw it into the black sewer pipe, where it skidded and echoed, and when Yoyo ran after it and disappeared, his barking and the scratching of his paws echoed back into the ditch, too. Like an Indian slipping up behind a man bent over a spring, Alvin crept to the mouth of the sewer. Inside, Yoyo barked. Alvin felt cold. Some older boys had even crawled inside, underground to the creek. He bent over and looked into the tunneling blackness. Two points of red pulsed like the tubes in the back when you snap off the radio. "Whooot!" Alvin bellowed, and stepped back when the sewer went "whooooooo!" at *him*. He straightened up and listened against the wind in the trees for his mother's voice. The wind dropped, the trees were still, and he heard only silence.

"You'd be too chicken to hunt for no killer," Baby Jean had said. "I know *you*, Alvin Henderlight. You a-skeert of yer own shadder." He laughed, bug-eyed, like a monster. "The Shaaadooooow knoooooows." And then he mocked again the laugh they heard on the radio every evening last winter. Alvin had wished Baby Jean would pay more attention to his nose, and now he wiped his own to make sure. "Why, you even afraid to go in the sewer pipe," Baby Jean had said.

Yoyo came dimly into view at the mouth of the sewer. One night Alvin learned that he would always be afraid of the dark. When the sun was a crooked square of soft yellow on the wallpaper, Gran'maw held him up so he could look down at Gran'paw. He was such a little man that they had to lay him out in Alvin's barred bed, reluctant until the last moment to put him in the wooden coffin. In the cream-yellow baby bed by the radio, Gran'paw was dressed up in black, his hands on his chest as if he were smoothing down his lapels, and his face white as pie dough. So they had had to figure out a place for Alvin to sleep.

He had ended up in the deep clothes box that smelled of moth balls and musty cotton in the bedroom where Gran'paw and Gran'maw used to sleep together. It was the coal-blackest place he had ever been, and he kept worrying, afraid the heavy wooden lid would come crashing down over him. But he had been afraid to cry loud because it still seemed that he would wake Gran'-paw. A soft-spoken man, he would go for his belt if any of the children disturbed him. They would lie on the dust-choky rug under the radio, the yellow wax dial glowing mellow, and looking up in the dim light see Gran'paw, rocking in the wicker chair, his small feet hardly touching the figured rug, holding his brown leather belt in one hand and a White Owl in the other, while Major Bowes' deep voice on "The Amateur Hour" that made Alvin sleepy throbbed out of the radio, and if they heard the wicker chair creak suddenly, Alvin and whatever cousin was there knew they had whispered too loud and were in for it.

His hand on the holster, he was on his knees on the lip of the sewer, looking into the living blackness, even before the decision took shape in his mind. If you always tracked a killer down in the dark, you couldn't be afraid of the dark to begin with. The harsh, grainy concrete cut through his knickers into his knees. The palms of his hands ached and burned as he pulled himself through the tunnel with frog-like motions. The sooty darkness ahead was deeper, hummed with a more final silence, than that room four or five years ago. But the holster flapped gently on his hip, and looking over his shoulder he saw Yoyo's eyes like the radio tubes.

The dry hiss of the toes of his shoes as he crawled was worse than the hollow, numb ringing of the silence in his ears. He thought of the jungle outside, the red clay, the brown dewberry and blackberry vines, the trees blowing in the chilly wind, and imagined he heard his mother calling him, but he knew that the tunnel and the outside were deaf to each other. Yoyo's hairy flank brushed past Alvin's shoulder. Even with his own dog, even with one of the big boys, Baby Jean would be afraid to crawl three feet. Knowing that, knowing that if he could make it to the creek and the daylight, he would never be afraid of Baby Jean again, Alvin scraped ahead on his knees. Over his shoulder, the entrance curved behind him, looking, at its mouth, like the bore hole in the muzzle of his daddy's hunting rifle. His knees were wet, dampness seeped into his bones, little needling red specks danced in the darkness, and in his throat, he felt the thudding of his heart and heard it beat in his ears. He looked back again. The bead of light was blacked out. In the black whirl behind him, he imagined the sudden onrush of snakes, spiders, rats, flood, and debris.

Suddenly, a maniac's laugh rumbled toward him, then swallowed him like hoops of echoes: "The Shaaadooooow knooooows. Whooooo whooowhowho!" Alvin's teeth broke the chapped skin and he tasted salt.

He turned in the fluid darkness of the narrow pipe. Yoyo's barking rolled over him. The cement skinned his head and his crazy bone struck it. He tried to stifle the scream that gurgled in his throat as he crawled, a crippled, scurrying thing. Light struck his eyes, and he fell on his face in the ditch. He screamed, loud, long, feeling the tension ebb, tears moistening his sore eyes.

Yoyo jumped out of the ditch and loped into the jungle. Alvin's breath stopped rasping through his throat. Under his stomach he was wet. But when he touched the water with his hand, he knew it was from the ditch and stopped feeling ashamed. He got up on his knees. The wind didn't stir. He stood up and leaned against the wall. The rocks felt good, sharp. He heard the weeds move, but the hedgeberries were still as BBs.

He looked over the edge of the ditch. Through the weeds and looped briars, he saw something red flash at the edge of the trunk of a sycamore. He glanced quickly left. Black hair moved in the weeds. Something moved on the right, but he missed it. Then he heard the laugh. The hedge moved behind him. He spun around. The green berries moved and the wind chilled his hot cheeks. But on the other side of the ditch something else made the weeds whisper and move. Then boys' whispering, louder than the grass. Broken behind the stalks of young trees, someone crawled across the red clay. The laugh came from the left, it rose louder, nearer, on the right, and in front of Alvin, Baby Jean's voice filtered through the weeds. "The Shaaaadoooow knooooows." All three laughed. Then nothing moved.

Suddenly, Yoyo shot up out of the briars and ran barking around the jungle. Boys jumped up, screaming like Indians, and ran toward the ditch waving pistols. Baby Jean led the running, the laughing, and the screaming, while Yoyo circled them, barking, and Alvin ran down the ditch toward the street. He didn't understand what they were yelling until he hit the macadam where a woman was taking clothes off a line in the yard by the street and knew he was safe. "Hey, Alvin! It was *me* killed your gran'paw!" "Me, me, *I* did it, Alvin!" "*He* did it, Alvin!" "Shut up, men! It was meeeeee! The Shadooooow!" yelled Baby Jean until his face turned red. Alvin turned and walked toward home, trying not to run. "Stay out of our jungle—or we'll shoot you like we shot your gran'paw!"

Momma's white De Soto wasn't parked by the fire plug.

The front door was locked. He wiggled the tips of his fingers along the rusty bottom of the mailbox, got the key, unlocked the door. The living room was cold. The fire in the grate had died to gray dust. The cat looked up from sleeping on the dead radio. Loudly, the kitchen clock ticked. The feeling that came over him in the sewer pipe tried to come back. On the oilcloth on the table lay a note.

Alvin. Don't you go off. You stay right here. We'll be back about 5. And you can count on a good whipping for not minding me. Momma.

"Huh!" That always buffaloed him. What was a *good* whipping?

He looked through the kitchen window at the huge shaggy hedge that, higher than Uncle Bud's head, surrounded the house. Leaning on the sill, his nose and mouth pressed flat against the chilled pane, he recalled how Gran'maw told it: "Well, way it was, the principal sent Bud home one day with this note to gran'daddy, sayin, 'Mr. Willis, your boy has acted up in arithmetic class again an looks like I'm goin to have to give him a first-class whippin tomorrow. You are expected to be present when I administer it.' Well, come next morning an Freddie said, 'Bud, go out in the yard and cut two big strong switches off the hedge.' Bud did. Then Freddie, no taller than Bud was in the sixth grade, took Bud's hand and off they went to school. 'Here I am,' Freddie told the principal. 'Come to watch you whup my boy. An I brung two switches.' 'How come two?'" he asked Freddie. 'One is for you to use on Bud an the other is for me to wear out on you when you're done.' " Alvin laughed, his mouth making a strange sound against the breath-frosted window pane. That story sure tickled the fool out of him, sometimes so bad he nearly wet his pants.

Then he felt guilty and ashamed. What would Gran'-paw think, looking down, and not seeing Alvin with Uncle Bud and Momma and Gran'maw around the grave? He'd be especially hurt, because hadn't everybody always said that Alvin took more after his gran'paw than even Uncle Bud? And to make Gran'paw feel even worse, there was only one thing to call a somebody who was afraid to go through the sewer to the creek, who ran out of the ditch. And how could somebody who was afraid to do that ever go out and hunt down—?

Walking back and forth through the rooms, his hands in his knickers' pockets, he tried to think of a way to make up for it. Sitting on the lowered lid of the toilet, he saw Uncle Bud's air rifle. He had gone off without hiding it from Alvin, had left it leaning in the corner outside the bathroom. Holding it, Alvin thought of shooting it a few times at the coal house, but he felt a sudden sense of power. And he knew what he could do.

Going into the living room, he glanced into the bedroom at the wooden clothes box that sat at the foot of Gran'maw's bed. He could do it now, and not have to wait until he was grown up, with it always on his mind, worrying him. His heart thudded, and the room seemed to shrink. He lifted the lid and dug beneath the spare quilts and his faded baby clothes, that always gave him a sad, nervous feeling to come upon, like the cream-yellow baby bed stored in the coal house. The scrapbook was on the very bottom. Why did old people always seem to be hiding everything?

It didn't take long to find it. But the mice had chewed most of the printing off the clipping so only the pictures remained. Beside the picture of Gran'paw was a face he hadn't remembered. A lean, dark face like a mean man in the Johnny Mack Brown chapter play. He cut the picture out with his jack-knife. He was about to let the lid fall when he saw the shoes. Once Gran'maw had shown them to him, saying, "They still in good shape. Won't be long fore you'll be able to wear um, they so small." He sat down beside the box and tried them on. They felt a fit. He threw his own wet shoes onto the back porch.

He had the rifle and dry shoes and determination but nowhere to begin looking. Then he remembered Uncle Bud telling how he ran off one day when Gran'paw whipped him, struck out down the railroad tracks and along about dark he was cold and scared and he looked up and there was a lumber yard, and who was it but Gran'paw coming through the gate and saw him standing there on the rail, trying to get his balance, his mouth wide open.

Then that's what *he* would do. If it weren't for the seat sticking up and having to lug the air rifle he could take the Western Flyer. He wished the air rifle were a pistol so he could carry it in the holster. He locked the door, dropped the key in the mailbox, and walked toward the railroad tracks where the semaphore was green.

He tried to stay on the rail, but kept losing his balance. The shoes were too large. The crossties were too far apart, and walking on the rocks wore him out, so he ended up on the black cinders that got in his shoes. He kept having to sit down and shake them out, something he reckoned Dick Tracy never had to do. *He* had a car to go in, and here Alvin was having to leg it.

As he walked, he decided perhaps he better not kill the murderer. Momma once told him, "They put you in the 'lectric chair even if all you do is kill a murderer." Once he found out where he lived from the lumber yard, Alvin would just put in a call to the police, they'd come and capture him, with Alvin's help, and cart him off and put him so far *under* the jail he'd never see daylight again. But he wished they weren't so strict about killing guys like that.

When he got tired of counting the ties, he began counting the telephone poles. He could vaguely remember. He was only three years old and he and his cousin Kenneth were wearing sun suits, sitting in Gran'paw's car where they weren't supposed to be, and Kenneth was fiddling with all the instruments when he pushed one button too many. The car started to roll down the slope. Just as he heard Momma somewhere behind him scream, the wide open door caught on the telephone pole and the car stopped. Momma was crying and stripping a hedge switch to use on them, but Gran'paw was at the car by then and yelled up to her, "Don't you touch them youn'uns! Just be glad they still alive!" And that same day, they went on a picnic to the Smoky Mountains, and the clearest picture he had of his gran'paw was when Alvin was sitting in the thick heat of the back seat of the car, the car parked in the alley now, watching Gran'paw walk down the back yard in the bright glare of the sun, lugging a freezer full of homemade banana ice cream that he always churned hard as jaw breakers, then he would beat his own serving with a spoon until it got soupy and eat it with cold cornbread and make the women have to turn their heads.

He had wandered through Knoxville before, but not this far. Familiar things faded behind him and strange things loomed ahead. Those hills the railroad cut through might be Lonsdale, and over there must be Southern Railway Shops. No doubt that was the biggest place he had ever seen. More trains in one place than he ever imagined existed and smoke coming black out of chimneys five times higher than Gran'maw's house, curling into the sky against the raw red, orange, and yellow of the sunset, smudging the sun where it set on the crest of the ridges. He dreaded to think of how lonely everything would look after the sun was gone behind the ridge and the last dying streak of smoky red died.

Up on a hill, beyond the dirty red, gray, and black buildings of the factories, stood houses that were like coal shacks. Upon the windows pulsed a pale orange warm glow, and all the chimneys let out smoke as though they did it together.

His hands, ears, and nose were cold. His shoes were full of cinders that cut his cold feet as the concrete had cut his palms in the tunnel. The air rifle was getting heavier with every step. He wished he had waited until he was a little older.

On the hill, at his back now, a woman in an apron came out onto a back porch, cupped her hands to her

mouth: "Herrrrrrrmannnnn! Herman! You get you'-
self home, you hear?" She sounded angry but sad. He
imagined Herman trapped in a sewer pipe.

He wished he had heard Momma calling. But he had
been underground then, worming through that sewer.
They told how Gran'paw used to go out and stand in
the back yard and holler for Uncle Bud to come on in
for supper, and Uncle Bud, curb-hopping at Harper's
drug store, would hear him all the way through the
woods, across the creek to Broadway, and Bud would
come running. There was something about that Alvin
liked—Uncle Bud running as soon as he was called. Alvin's daddy never whipped him, never got mad at him,
and he didn't know why, but that made him feel uneasy.

So weak and tired he could hardly set one heavy foot
before the other now, he sat on the rail and felt the weariness, like a liquid, pervade his body. He shot two BBs
into a box-car. The cold rail trembled under his buttocks.
A train was coming hellfire toward him. He jumped as
though a wasp had bitten him. As the train passed, waves
of wind and noise throbbed against him. He watched the
faded red caboose shrink too small to see. Shivering,
looking around, he peed against the rail. Then he saw
stacks of lumber, sky high.

The gate was chained and locked. He stared at it, weary,
trying to think. Everybody had already gone home, except maybe the night watchman. *He* would know. Alvin would show him the man's picture.

It was such a huge lumber yard that Alvin decided
he'd better not just stand there waiting for the night
watchman to pass. The sun was gone, dark coming on.
Smelling the raw lumber, he went through the weeds
around the barbed wire fence, looking through the gaps

in the stacks of lumber for the watchman to appear. He
saw a househigh pile of sawdust and faintly felt a sense
of the fun it would be to play in it with Baby Jean, but
that faded.

When he saw the hole in the barbed wire, he didn't
hesitate. Going in, walking among the high stacks of lumber, looking for the watchman, he began to feel afraid.
He didn't know how he'd be able to say it. And if the
man could tell him where the murderer lived, it would
be full dark then, and colder, and he would be hungrier
than he was now.

The picture, the one that made him love his gran'paw
more than anything else did, came to mind again. In
glowing sunlight, he was sitting back in a chair, braced
against the wall, wearing a light hat, a dark vest, gray
striped trousers with that wide brown belt and the gun
and holster, and you could see the tops of the very shoes
Alvin was now wearing because Gran'paw had his feet
resting on the rungs of the chair: a little chubby man with
a soft face, a gentle, sad mouth and misty eyes that looked
out of the picture at you as though he were wondering
why in the world you ever wanted to take a picture of
him. What was clearest of all in the picture now was
Gran'paw holding a big bottle of sweet milk in one hand
and a marshmallow cookie with coconut on it in the other,
and the picture was snapped right here in the lumber
yard.

He tried to find a piece of paper lying around. If he
didn't do it soon it would be too late and he surely didn't
want to end up smelling like Baby Jean. The door into
the little building wasn't locked. If the night watchman
was sitting in there having his supper, he might have
some leftovers. But first, Alvin would have to ask where

the bathroom was. He turned the white porcelain knob and went in.

In the light that came very faintly through the grimy window panes were a desk, with papers on it, a light bulb hanging down, cabinets and chairs, and at the rear a closed door. The air rifle clashed against an iron box, SAFE printed on the door. He opened the rear door, and the rim of a toilet bowl gleamed in the sudden light.

He shut the door, laid the rifle across the sink, let his knickers drop around his ankles, and slowly sat down. The seat was cold as a curbstone. He shivered, surrounded by lumber, miles and miles of strange houses and streets between him and home. He wished he had never left. His stomach growled with emptiness and hurt. He bit his chapped lip, straining. But he couldn't. At first the tears were from effort, but then he was trembling, and a dry hissing sound came from his mouth as he cried with sudden helplessness and hopelessness.

He heard the door open and in the same moment looked up. He was so startled by the man's face in the pallid light that when his body relaxed in the moment before the startle and the recoil of terror, it happened, and he even felt the brief relief before he saw the gun in the murderer's hand, pointed at him. There was the first sound, the one he made himself, then the pause, and then, just as the terror began, another sound, this time from the lean, dark-faced man. He was laughing, the pistol lowered at his side now, and Alvin thought he was going to say, "The Shaaaaadooow knoooows."

"Don't shoot me, mister. I won't say a word about it!"

"About what?" The man could hardly talk through the laughter.

"You know. But I swear to goodness I won't tell a soul—if you only just won't shoot me."

"Why, son, id take a mighty mean feller to shoot a man in the fix *you're* in. You get done your bizness an don't worry. How the hell you git in y'ere anyhow?"

Now Alvin couldn't speak, caught in a humiliation he never dreamt possible. The man laughed again and shut the door. Quickly, Alvin took the clipping from his shirt pocket. Sure as the world, the same man. He looked around for some paper. A bare roll hung on the wall. He used the clipping. After he'd gotten his pants buckled, he felt better, even a little less of a baby. He had to do something though, now that the man knew.

Aiming the air rifle at the door, he listened to the man talk to someone on the telephone. And waited. When his arms grew too tired to hold up the air rifle, he had to let them down and that was when the door opened again. But the man grabbed the barrel before Alvin could raise it. He took it from him and pulled Alvin into the office and told him to sit down in one of the swivel chairs and be still.

"Now whur you live, son?" Calling him 'son' sounded strange. He wanted to know so he could go and kill Momma and Gran'maw and Uncle Bud, too. But that was one thing Alvin wouldn't do, no matter what.

"Okay. No worry a mine. Let *them* take care of it." He had called his men to come help him. They were going to torture him to tell. Alvin jumped from the chair and right into the suddenly open arms of the man and the smell of his breath that reminded him of Baby Jean as he forced Alvin back into the chair. The man sat across from him, watching him in the dim light.

When a car horn blew outside, the old man rose and said, "Come on with me, boy." Alvin's air rifle jogged at his side. Alvin walked ahead of him through the lumber yard to the gate where a car was parked. He recognized the brown and yellow of a police car. When he saw one, he always sang, 'A tisket a tasket, a brown and yellow basket,' but he didn't now. He was confused. He couldn't fit everything together. But he was so tired he could hardly keep his eyes from blinking and the high stacks of lumber made him dizzy.

One policeman stood at the gate, smiling. Another sat in the car, in the dark.

"What in the world was he doin in *there?*" the one at the gate asked.

"Looks like the boy they reported missin," said the one in the car.

"The one *what?*"

The policeman outside and the killer were laughing now. He wished they would stop it.

"He kilt my gran'paw when he wasn't lookin."

"Is that a fact? How bout that—did you kill this boy's gran'paw?"

The other policeman got into the car beside Alvin now, still laughing. The old man came to the door on the driver's side and leaned in. "I don't even know who the *youn'un* is, much less his gran'paw."

"My gran'paw's Freddie Willis an you shot him in the back."

The three men were silent for a moment and Alvin felt a swell of triumph. But when they started laughing again, he verged on crying.

"Well, I'll be dadburn!" said the old man. "I reckon

they have to tell a youn'un *somethin*, but that's a hell of a thing to throw off on *me*."

"What's you talkin about anyway?" the policeman behind the wheel asked.

"Not in front of the boy. Tell you later sometime. But now you listen to me, son. Your gran'daddy was my best friend. I's the one found him. He—well, you just remember that, an tell your gran'maw I said I sure don't appreciate it."

"Thanks for callin," the policeman said, starting the motor.

"This here air rifle's his'n, too." He handed it across the driver and Alvin. The other policeman took it.

The car turned and drove away through strange streets. He didn't even ask why they didn't arrest the old man. He was too confused and cold and hungry and sleepy, and he didn't trust them as far as he could throw a rock.

He awoke in Gran'maw's room in coal-blackness. When he opened his eyes, he saw tiny red dots jiggling upon the black velvet dark. Muffled laughter came through the door. Then he distinguished Momma's voice and then Gran'maw's and Uncle Bud's, all talking at once it seemed, and sounding gay. Wanting to hear, to know what made them laugh, he got out of bed, staggered sleepily across the cold floor and put his ear against the door.

"Reminds me of the time," Gran'maw was saying, "they used to tell about Freddie when he's little—runnin off that time. Only tin years old an he ended up in Chattanooga. Went all that way by one means an t'uther an the police picked him up wanderin the streets way early one mornin, and they took him in an kept him at the station house three days fore they got hold of his paw an put him on the train home. Chief wrote an told how Freddie was such a little gentleman the whole time. An Freddie wrote him a letter thankin him in the most high-tone terms for treatin him so good."

"You still got that clipping that told about daddy runnin off, Momma?" asked Momma.

Gran'maw said, "Wouldn't let that get lost for the world. Got it in the album in the clothes box."

"Momma, you think we ought to tell Alvin what really happened?" asked Alvin's Momma.

"Shoot fire, no! He's too little to hear such as that. Can't bear thinkin of it myself, let alone a eight year old boy that'd do what he done today out of love for his gran'daddy he hardly even knowed."

"I remember," Uncle Bud said, "it took me a long time to figure out what suicide meant. But I was thirteen an oughta known by then."

Alvin stood a few moments longer on the bare, cold floor. Groping through the blackness toward the bed, he struck his knee against a sharp corner of the clothes box. But as he crawled into bed and under the covers, the ringing pain slowly ebbed. Then he knew they'd heard him. The door opened and Momma stood darkly with a floor of light behind her. She seemed at the end of a long hallway. As she came toward him, her body merging with the darkness, the words formed in his mind, but when she tucked the covers tightly over his shoulders and he felt her thick hair graze his hot cheek, the question faded for a night.

The Day the Flowers Came

J. D. OPENED his eyes. A woman was talking to him. A man began talking to him. Through the pain in his head, in his eyes, he saw his own living-room ceiling. Who were these people? Why was he on the couch? On the coffee table sat an empty Jack Daniel's fifth and two glasses. Why two? The voices went on talking to him. "Yes?" he asked.

Chimes. As he raised himself up to answer the front door, a magazine slipped off his chest and flopped onto the pale-rose carpet. *True.* Light through the wide window clashed on his eyes. The chimes. He stumbled to the wall, pulled the drape cord, darkened the room. Light flickered from the television set in the corner. The man and the woman who had been talking to him were talking to each other in a family situation-comedy series. The husband was greeting a neighbor at the door. But J. D. still heard chimes.

Going to the door, he wondered why he wasn't at the office. Labor Day. Where were Carolyn? Ronnie? Ellen?

The sudden smell of flowers, thrust at him in red profusion as he opened the door, made J. D. step back. "Carolyn, flowers!" No, she was gone. With the kids.

"This the Hindle residence?"

"My wife's in Florida."

Taking the basket the young man reverently handed

75

him, J. D. tried to remember whose birthday or anniversary fell on Labor Day.

As the young man started back down the walk toward his truck, J. D. read the printed message: *"My deepest sympathy."*

As though he had blundered into a stranger's private grief, J. D. yelled, "Hey, come back here, fella."

"Something wrong?"

"Yeah, I'm afraid you've got the wrong house."

"You *are* Mr. Hindle, aren't you?"

"Yes, but you must have the wrong Hindle," said J. D., his tone expressing respect for the anonymous dead. "There's been no death in *this* family."

J. D. handed the young man the basket. He took it and walked back to his truck.

Sunlight on endless roofs below glared up at J. D. as he paused a moment on his porch, which was at the crest of a roll in the Rolling Hills Homes community. Blinking, he went in and turned off the TV, picked up the bottle and the glasses and started to the kitchen to find coffee. As he passed the front door, the chimes sounded.

The young man again with the flowers.

"I checked and double-checked, Mr. Hindle. They're for you."

"Listen, nobody died here. The card's unsigned and the whole thing's a mistake. OK?" J. D. shut the door and went on to the kitchen. Through the window over the sink, he saw the delivery boy get into his truck without the flowers.

They stood on the porch, red, fresh, redolent. About to leave them there, J. D. saw a familiar car come down the street, so he took the roses and set them just inside the door.

Every morning since they had moved into this house three years ago, J. D. had found coffee in the pot as dependably as he had seen daylight in the yard. This morning, daylight hung full and bright in the young birch tree, but the pot was empty. When he found the coffee, he realized he didn't know how to operate the new-model percolator. When he finally found the instant coffee, he was exhausted. The drinking he had done last night had a double impact because it had been solitary, depressing.

Now, how did the damned *stove* work? The latest model, it left him far behind. The kitchen was a single, integrated marvel—or mystery—princess pink. The second outfit since they had built the house. For Carolyn, it had every convenience. On the rare occasions when J. D. entered the kitchen, he simply dangled in the middle of the room, feeling immersed in a glimmer of pink that was, this morning, a hostile blur.

He let the hot water in the bathroom washbowl run, filled the plastic, insulated coffee mug, spooned instant coffee from the jar into the cup and stirred, viciously. The first sip scalded his tongue; the second, as he sat on the edge of the tub, made him gag. Perhaps three teaspoonfuls was too much.

In the hall he slipped on Ronnie's plastic puzzle set strewn over the already slickly polished floor, and the pain of hot coffee that spilled down the front of his shirt made him shudder.

His feeling of abandonment seemed more intense than his feeling of contentment yesterday as he watched Carolyn and the kids board the plane. Sitting on the couch, he tried to see their faces.

Chimes startled him.

A different deliveryman stood on the porch, holding a green urn of lilies, using both hands, though his burden looked light.

"What do you want?"

"You J. D. Hindle?"

"Yes."

"Flowers."

"In God's name, what *for?*"

"I think there's a card."

J. D. set the coffee cup on the hall table and took a card out of its tiny white envelope: "*We extend our deepest sympathy to you in your recent bereavement. James L. Converse, Manager, Rolling Hills Homes.*"

"Wait a moment, will you?"

Leaving the man holding the lilies, J. D. went to the telephone in a confusion of anger and bewilderment and dialed Converse's number. His office didn't answer. Labor Day. His home didn't answer. Gone fishing, probably.

"Everything OK?"

"I can take a joke," said J. D., taking the flowers. Good ol' Bill Henderson must be working on his masterpiece, thought J. D. Not just one more stupid practical joke. He's putting *everything* into this one. He tipped the deliveryman. He set the lilies beside the roses.

But as he showered, the more he thought about it, the less he felt *inclined* to take a joke like this.

Out of razor blades. In this world's-fair deluxe bathroom exhibit, he knew there was a blade dispenser concealed in the fixtures somewhere. When he found it, he would probably be delightfully amazed. Since Carolyn always saw to it that his razor was ready, he had had no occasion to use the dispenser. But he remembered it as one of the bathroom's awesome features. He pushed a button. Pink lotion burped out onto his bare toes. He ripped a Kleenex out of a dispenser under the towel cabinet. It seemed that the house, masterfully conceived to dispense with human beings, had not really existed for him until this morning, now that its more acclimatized human beings had temporarily vacated it.

Where were his underclothes, his shirts, his trousers—which Carolyn had waiting for him on the mobile valet gizmo every morning? In the first three houses they had had—each representing a major step in the insurance company's hierarchy—he had known where most things were and how to operate the facilities. He remembered vividly where his shirts used to hang in the house in Greenacres Manor. As second vice-president, perhaps he spent more time away now, more time in the air. Coming home was more and more like an astronaut's re-entry problem.

His wrist watch informed him that two hours had been consumed in the simple act of getting up and dressing himself—in lounging clothes, at that. As he entered the living room again, he heard a racket in the foyer. When he stepped off the pale-rose carpet onto the pinkish marble, water lapped against the toe of his shoe. The roses lay fanned out on the marble. A folded newspaper, shoved through the brass delivery slot, lay on the floor. When J. D. picked it up, water dripped on his trousers.

He removed the want-ad section and the comics and spread them over the four-branched run of water, stanching its flow.

He wished the chill of autumn had not set in so firmly. How nice it would be to sit on the veranda and read the morning paper leisurely in the light that filtered through the large umbrella. He opened the drapes a little and sat in his black-leather easy chair. The cold leather chilled him thoroughly. He would have to turn the heat on.

On page two, as he clucked his tongue to alleviate the bitterness of the second cup of instant coffee on the back of his tongue, he read a news report twice about the death of Carolyn Hindle, 36, and her children, Ronald H. Hindle, 7, and Ellen Hindle, 9, in a hurricane near Daytona Beach, Florida. Survived by J. D. Hindle, 37, vice-president of——

"I'm sorry, all lines to Florida are in use."

"But, operator, this is an emergency."

"Whole sections of the Florida coast, sir, are in a state of emergency. Hurricane Gloria——"

"I *know* that! My wife——"

"And with Labor Day. . . . Do you wish me to call you when I've contacted the Breakers Hotel, or do you wish to place the call later?"

"Call me."

J. D. flicked on the television and gulped the cold instant coffee. It was a mistake. They had mistakenly listed survivors instead of victims. Or perhaps they were only—the phone rang—missing.

"Mr. Hindle, on your call to the Breakers Hotel in Florida, the manager says that no one by the name of Carolyn Hindle is registered there."

"Well, she *was* a little uncertain in her plans."

"She didn't say exactly where she would be staying?"

"No, she left rather impulsively, but—— Listen, could you ask if she *has* been there?"

"I did, sir. She hasn't."

That opened up the entire state of Florida. On television, games and old movies, but no word of the hurricane. He would have to take the day off and try, some-how, perhaps through the Red Cross, to track her and the children down. Chimes.

On the porch stood the first delivery boy, long-stemmed roses again in a basket.

"This time I'm certain, Mr. Hindle."

J. D. accepted them. On the card was written in lovely script: "*They are just away. Our heartfelt sympathy. The Everlys.*"

J. D. picked up the roses that had spilled, put them in their basket and hooked both baskets of roses over his arms and carried the urn of lilies with them into the living room. Still, there was something wrong. Flowers so soon, so quickly? He looked up the newspaper's phone number and dialed it.

"I'm just the cleaning lady, mister. They put out the paper, then locked up tight."

Just as J. D. placed the receiver in its cradle, the ring-ing phone startled him.

"Mr. J. D. Hindle?"

"Yes."

"Western Union. Telegram."

"Read it, will you?"

"Dearest Jay: The kids and I are having wonderful, wonderful time. We all miss you. But we may return sooner than planned. Love and kisses, Carolyn, Ronnie and Ellen."

"I knew it, I knew it! God, God. . . . When was that telegram sent?"

"This morning."

"What time, exactly?"

"Hour ago. Eight o'clock. You want me to mail it?"

"What?"

"Some people like to keep a record."

"Yes. Please do. And thank you very much."

The flowers smelled like spring now and he bent over them and inhaled, his eyes softly closed. Then, glancing down at the newspaper on the floor, he became angry. He dialed the home of the editor of the suburban paper.

"Are you certain?"

"Listen, Mr. Garrett, it's *your* accuracy that's being questioned. That telegram was dated today and sent an hour ago. Now, I want to know where your information came from. What town? Why? This house is full of flowers."

"Well, if we're in error, Mr. Hindle, we'll certainly print a correction in tomorrow's paper. Meanwhile, I'll investigate the matter inmmediately and call you back when I've tracked something down."

"I'll be waiting."

Chimes. J. D. picked up the flowers again and carried them to the door. The odor was good, but they breathed all the oxygen, and the overtone of funerals still emanated from them. He would unload them all on whichever deliveryman it was *this* time.

Bill Henderson stood on the porch holding a tray covered with a white cloth. "Nancy sent you something hot, Jay."

"That was sweet of her, Bill. Excuse me." J. D. set the flowers outside on the porch. "Come in." J. D. was smiling. He was aware that Bill noticed he was smiling.

"We were about to risk our lives on the freeway today, to visit Nancy's people, when we saw the newspaper. Jay, I—"

"Thanks, Bill, but save it. It's a mistake. A stupid mistake. I just heard from Carolyn."

"What? You mean she's OK? She called?"

"Yes. Well, she sent a telegram from Florida an hour ago. Didn't even mention the hurricane."

"That's odd. Must be on everybody's *mind* down there."

"Yeah, a little inconsiderate, in a way. She might know I'd be worried about that."

"Maybe the telegram was delayed. The hurricane and all."

"What're you trying to say?"

"Nothing."

"Why can't it be the *newspaper* that's wrong?"

"Well, it just doesn't seem likely."

"Look, let's shut up about it, OK? I've got a hangover from drinking alone last night."

"Why didn't you call me? We could have had a few hands of poker."

"Yeah. Why didn't I? It was a strange night. And now all this flood of flowers this morning. My stomach's in knots. You know, at first there, Bill, with the flowers and all, I even got it in my head that it might have been one of your sick jokes." The look of astonishment that came instantly to Bill's face made J. D. add quickly, "But when I saw the piece in the paper, I knew how stupid I—"

"My God, J. D., you think I'd do a terrible thing like that for laughs?"

"That's what I'm trying to get across to you. I feel damn guilty for even *thinking* . . . . Well, I sure gave that editor hell. He'll be calling back in a little bit. Listen, have a cup of coffee with me before you hit the highway."

"OK, then I guess we may's well go ahead with our trip."

Lifting the white cloth from the tray, J. D. felt an

eerie sensation in his stomach that the sight of the smoking food dispelled. "I'm going to eat this anyway, OK? Not enough coffee for both of us. You have this and I'll make some more instant for myself."

Running the water in the bathroom basin again, waiting for it to get steaming hot, J. D. heard the telephone ring.

"Hey, Bill, you mind getting that for me?"

J. D. spooned coffee into the plastic mug and watched it stain the water. Steam rising made his eyes misty. Bill was a blur in the bathroom door. J. D. blinked the tears from his eyes. Bill's face was grimly set.

"What's the matter with *you*?"

"That was the editor. He thought I was you, so he started right in with his report. Listen, let's go in the living room."

"Hell with the living room. What did he *say*?"

"The story . . . . checks out . . . . through Associated Press. Jay, I'm sorry. . . ."

"Bill," said J. D., looking straight into his eyes. "What are you doing here?"

"What do you mean, Jay?"

"I mean, how is it you came in right after the newspaper arrived?"

"Listen, Jay, you know here lately, you've been—"

"It wouldn't be because you wanted to see how it was getting to me, would it, Bill? I mean, you're not *that* goddamned—"

"Jay, you better get out of this house. You're not used to being alone here."

"I've got to find out what the hell's going on here!"

"Nancy and I'll stay home," said Bill, backing out of the bathroom. "You come on over with me and—"

"Look, just leave me alone, Bill."

"Jay, if you think I—"

"I don't know, I don't know anything. But if you did, I fell for it, okay? All the way. I'm still sick, I'll *be* sick all day."

"I'm not leaving, Jay, as long as you've got it in your head—"

"All right! It's a mistake! Some cruel mix-up somewhere! But leave me alone, will you?"

"Yeah, I think I'd better go, Jay." Bill walked out, leaving the front door open.

J. D. flopped onto the couch. The mixture of emotions that had convulsed him was now a vivid anger without a target. Seeing the tray of food, no longer steaming, on the footrest of his leather chair, he leaped to his feet and took the tray into the bathroom and with precise flips of his wrist, tossed the eggs, toast, coffee, jelly, butter and bacon into the toilet and flushed it. Over the sound of water, he heard the chimes.

With the tray still in his hands, he went into the foyer, where the door still stood open. Among the flowers he had set out on the porch stood a woman, smartly dressed. She held a soup tureen in both gloved hands. The sight of the tray surprised her and she smiled awkwardly, thinking, perhaps, that she had come at the end of a line and that J. D. was ready for her. She started to set the tureen on the tray, saying, "I'm Mrs. Merrill, president of your P. T. A., and I just want you to know—" But J. D. stepped back and lowered the tray in one hand to his side.

"A stupid, criminal mistake has been made here, Mrs. Merrill. I won't need the soup, thank you. Come again when my wife is home. They're having a wonderful time in Florida."

"With that horrible hurricane and all?"

"Yes, hurricane and *all*."

J. D. shut the door and turned back and locked it.

He closed the drapes and lay down on the couch again. His head throbbed as though too large for his body. Just as his head touched the cushion, the telephone rang. He let it. Then, realizing that it might be Carolyn, calling in person, he jumped up. It stopped before he could reach it. As he returned to the couch, it started again. Maybe she was finally worried about the hurricane, about *his* worrying about it.

"Hello."

"Is this the Hindle residence?"

"Yes . . ."

"May I speak with the lady of the house, please?"

"She isn't at home."

"May I ask when she *will* be?"

"Who is this, please?"

"My name is Janice Roberts, Mr. Hindle, and I'm with Gold Seal Portrait Studios. We *are* going to be *in* the Rolling Hills area in a few weeks, and your name has been selected for a special award."

"Miss—"

"For half price you may obtain a family portrait, either eight by ten or ten by twelve, and now, all we ask *of* you is that you tell your friends—"

J. D. slammed the receiver into its cradle.

Chimes. J. D. just stood there, letting the sound rock him like waves at sea. Among the flowers that crowded the porch stood the first delivery boy.

"If you touch those chimes one more time. . . ."

"Listen, mister, I'm only doing what I was told."

"*I'm* telling you—" Unable to finish, J. D. jerked the basket of flowers from the young man's hands and threw

it back at him. He turned and ran down the walk, and
J. D. kicked at the other baskets, urns and pots, until all
the flowers were strewn over the lawn around the small
porch.

He slammed the door and locked it again. Standing
on a chair, he rammed his fist against the electric-chimes
mechanism that was fastened to the wall above the front
door. The blow started the chimes going. He struck again
and again, until the pain in his hand made him stop.

Reeling about the house searching for an object with
which to smash the chimes, J. D. saw in his mind images
from a Charlie Chaplin movie he had seen on the late
show one night in the early years of television: Charlie
entangled in modern machinery on an assembly line. The
film moved twice as fast in his head. He found no deadly
weapon in the house nor in the garage that adjoined the
house. Seeing the switch box, he cut off the current.

Lying on the couch again, he tried to relax. He thought
of people passing, of more people coming to offer their
condolences, of the flowers strewn like gestures of in-
sanity in the yard. Carolyn would be shocked at the
stories she would hear of the flowers in the yard; for
until they all knew the truth, it would appear to the
neighbors that J. D. had no respect, no love, felt no remorse.

He went out and gathered the flowers into one over-
flowing armful and took them into the house and laid
them in his leather easy chair. Then he brought in the
baskets, urns and pots.

He had heard that lying on the floor relaxed tense
muscles and nerves. He tried it. He lay on the carpet,
arms and legs sticking straight out. After a few shuddering sighs, he began to drift, to doze. He recalled the fu-

nerals of some of his friends. Somewhat as these people today had approached him, he had approached the wives and families of his departed friends. For the important families, he had attended to insurance details himself. How artificial, meaningless, ridiculous, even cruelly stupid it all seemed now.

Coldness woke him. The room was black dark. The cold odor of roses and lilies was so strong he had to suck in air to breathe. He rolled over on his belly and rose on his hands and knees, then, holding onto the couch, pulled himself up.

Weak and shivering, he moved across the floor as though on a deck that heaved and sank. When he pulled the cord, the drapes, like stage curtains, opened on icy stars, a luminous sky.

None of the light switches worked. Then he remembered throwing the main switch in the garage. Using matches, he inched along until he found the switch.

Perhaps if he ate something, to get strength.

In the refrigerator, stacks of TV dinners. The pink stove gleamed in the fluorescent light of the kitchen. The buttons and dials, like the control panel of an airplane, were a hopeless confusion.

He was astonished that the first week in September could be so cold. Perhaps it had something to do with the hurricanes. Arctic air masses or something. What did he know of the behavior of weather? Nothing. Where was the switch to turn on the electric heat? He looked until he was exhausted. Perhaps he had better get out of the house for a while.

Sitting behind the wheel, his hand on the ignition, he wondered where he could go. A feeling of absolute indecision overwhelmed him. The realm of space and time in which all possibilities lay was a white blank.

As he sat there, hand on key, staring through the windshield as if hypnotized by the monotony of a freeway at night, he experienced a sudden intuition of the essence of his last moments with Carolyn. Ronnie and Ellen in the back seat, Carolyn sat beside J. D., saying again what she had said in similar words for weeks and in silence for months, perhaps years, before that: "I must get away for a while. Something is happening to me. I'm dying, very, very slowly; do you understand that, Jay? Our life. It's the way we live, somehow the way we live." No, he had not understood. Not then. He had only thought, How wonderful to be rid of all of you for a while, to know that in our house you aren't grinding the wheels of routine down the same old grooves, to feel that the pattern is disrupted, the current that keeps the wheels turning is off.

The telephone ringing shattered his daze. He went into the house.

Seeing the receiver on the floor, he realized that he had only imagined the ringing of the phone. But the chimes were going. He opened the door. There was only moonlight on the porch. Then he remembered striking at the chimes with his fist. Something had somehow sparked them off again.

As he stood on the threshold of his house, the chimes ringing, he looked out over the rooftops of the houses below, where the rolling hills gave the development its name. From horizon to horizon, he saw only roofs, gleaming in moonlight, their television aerials bristling against the glittering stars. All lights were out, as though there had been a massive power failure, and he realized how long he must have slept. He looked for the man in the moon, but the moon appeared faceless. Then, with the chimes filling the brilliantly lighted house at his back, he gazed up at the stars; and as he began to see Carolyn's face and Ronnie's face and Ellen's face more and more clearly, snow began to fall, as though the stars had disintegrated into flakes.

Love Makes Nothing
Happen

*W*ALT knelt in the snow, leaned forward to rest his shoulder against the evergreen, and waited for the bear to reappear.

He did not dare move nearer the cub. Now and then, he shifted his keened sight from the slope of the mountain, up which the bear would have to climb from the bay, to the mouth of the cave where the cub was sitting, like a baby waiting for its bottle. Walt's back ached from waiting, but he had tracked the bear all day across the island, and he knew that it would return before the sky grew darker through the trees. Against his other shoulder, he let lean the rifle he had "borrowed" from the company arms room.

While he waited, he thought of all the things the impulsive hunting trip was supposed to make him forget. He thought of Belle and Jimmy and "Mike."

But for a while he forced himself to think of trivial things. What a joke it was—the contrast between the colonel's reception speech about Anchorage's being a frontier town and the first eager trip into it to find nothing very different from Knoxville, Tennessee. Mountains all around, except here vivid white with snow all during the brief days. And beyond them, no ancestral paradise like Cades Cove in the Smokies, nothing but the miles of barren wastes that had given him an eerie feeling as he looked down from the troop plane.

Fox Island. It wasn't really an island. The bear had waded across during the summer, and Walt had quickly paddled across, breaking the thin ice. No foxes. Only the huge Alaska brown bear and her cub, the old trapper Walt had seen on the shore, and himself. *I'm* the fox. He forced a smile.

Resurrection Bay. Well, the name fit, for today anyway—Easter. That was how he got the three days off. But he had come to kill, not to resurrect. He didn't want to leave the cub behind, but he knew he couldn't get it back to Seward. Kill *it*, too? He wished it weren't there, watching, waiting.

If he were an Eskimo, Walt wouldn't have to worry about the "baby." He had read about them in the country school in Cades Cove before his family, dispossessed by the Park Commission, had moved into the big city of Knoxville. Sometimes, if the baby was a girl, the Eskimos left it out on the snow plains to starve, or for the wolves to eat. "Mike" was part wolf and part something else.

Belle had few Eskimo ways that Walt could see clearly. She had never lived in an igloo. A shack in Moose Pass. She worked in the canneries. But her grandfather came from Point Barrow and was a craftsman. Now he made nothing, not even to sell to the G.I.'s. Still, Belle had strange ways, sometimes. She was part Eskimo and part something else.

"Mike" was a pup when Walt found him in the snow while on maneuvers near Moose Pass, a year ago. He had been hunting then, too; the C.O. fined him for unauthorized use of an M-1.

The convoy had stopped at Moose Pass for water. Belle was standing in the doorway of her shack. She gave him some canned milk for the pup, and called it "Mike" right away. When they ordered Walt back to the truck, she told him where to find her. She was a dishwasher in the PX at Elmendorf Air Force Base.

Realizing that he was no longer thinking of trivial things, Walt tried to plan what he would do if the rifle were to jam. But he saw *her* again, as he had seen her in the PX that first night. He remembered how she looked dressed in each new thing he bought her. After a while, she began to have happy moments. When she finally let him move into the basement with her, on his promise to help her finish building the house, she tore up the pictures of Mike, the airman from Brooklyn. Belle and Mike were still living in the basement of the unfinished house when Mike deserted her.

He heard a noise, but it was not like a bear climbing through the snow. Through a break in the trees, he saw a cub plane gliding down toward a landing in Seward. Jimmy loved planes, especially jets. But their Sunday visit to the base had not made him love Walt. He reminded Walt of himself as a kid in Cades Cove, that other mountain place of wild animals and ancient people, where he had dreamed of being a roaming adventurer like Jack London.

Jimmy still watched every move Walt and Belle made in the dark underground rooms. Not even giving him the dog "Mike" seemed to change anything enough to make Walt feel content. The boy knew he had a real father somewhere. That was what made Jimmy so moody and nervous, made him stand and look into the yard, or into the house of the woman next door.

He wondered what made Belle brood so much and refuse to go out. Maybe if he took her back to Moose Pass to visit her mother and her grandfather . . . No, it was the baby in her belly. She always looked at him as though she expected Walt to walk out the door and never come back. For the first time, he wondered whether he really intended to take her and Jimmy and the baby and Mike back with him to Cades Cove.

A noise in the snow on the slope snapped the question out of his mind, leaving a lucid bright space which the sight of the huge brown bear suddenly filled. He tensed himself like a fox.

Belle sat at the table in the kitchen, writing a letter to her mother in Moose Pass.

Her hand trembled as she scrawled the words across the unlined paper: "Dear Momma, I want to cum home for a while but—" The light was bad. The brief days were ending now at three o'clock, after only four hours of feeble light.

A terrific noise rattled the window pane, shattering the film of snow. She looked up out of the underground room at the small rectangle of sky, but saw no jet. "They're gone before they come," Mike used to say about the jets. He knew something about everything—except her.

"—the roads ar bed. Ar you sur you want me to cum?"

But Walt had gone over those roads in a jeep, had passed through Moose Pass to get to Seward. He would have left her off there if she had asked. Maybe he would leave her *here* someday, without asking anything. Besides, she couldn't take Jimmy. She still had *some* pride. But her grandfather had too much. And she couldn't leave Jimmy here, not and get away with it. Grandfather wasn't too proud for *that*, in the old days up north. Mother was one of three girls he had not taken out; boys were different. But in Anchorage they punish you for that. She never had such thoughts when Jimmy was born, and she and Mike were still living in the little green caboose in the field. Only now, since she had first felt the new baby and the fear had come over her.

And now, too, she wanted Jimmy gone, even though he had eyes like Mike. Maybe then Walt would stay, too, or take her with him to that place where the other mountains were.

But she was sorry about throwing the scissors. "Well, the boy needs discipline." That's what Mike always said. Grandfather used to say that too. She had been sewing a button on Walt's fatigue jacket, annoyed because she was awkward with a needle, unlike Grandfather or Mother, who had craftsman skill. But angry too, because Walt had come home with the rifle hidden under his green overcoat and had gotten up before six and had gone out into the black darkness to hunt a bear. Not for meat, as in the tales Grandfather used to tell by the dying fire in the famished winter night. Merely to kill it.

Jimmy had come in to tell her that Louise, the young blonde wife of the Air Force sergeant, had told him to chain "Mike" up or she would call the police to come for him. "Mike" . . . she always regretted having named him "Mike" when he was a pup. Every time Jimmy's voice calling the half-breed dog reached her in the basement rooms, she wished she had cut the *dog* with the scissors, instead. She thought of Mike, the man, laughing as he taught her how to jitterbug, singing naughty songs, drinking and making love with great lusty flourishes.

She had ordered Jimmy to chain him up and go deliver his papers, but he had cried, he had begged her to tell Louise "where to get off at." She didn't like Louise any better than she liked the dog. Louise was married, and *her* baby was all one blood and beautiful. But even if Belle were to go to her, Louise's eyes would accuse her of being an Eskimo, and she would not be able to speak. Even when she screamed at him to obey her, Jimmy kept crying, whining, "Mother," begging her to defend him and that mongrel with the wolf's eyes. When she flung the scissors, he threw his hand up in the air, almost as though he were imitating his father's funny salute. The blade stuck in his palm, stayed poised for a moment, the finger holes like steel-rimmed eyes staring at her.

He looked at her in stunned disbelief, an expression which startled her. It was so much like Mike's when she had told him he had put a baby in her. Then Jimmy turned and ran up the stairs to ground level. For a while she sat trembling, staring at the blood on the floor. Then quickly she rose, and with the fatigue jacket mopped up the spots of blood, tiny as nailheads.

She felt alone, forsaken in her guilt. Because it was Easter, she wrote to her mother to calm her nerves. Easter meant nothing to Grandfather, but she hoped he would listen to the letter too and think kindly of her. And why shouldn't he? He knew nothing of Jimmy and Mike and Walt and this new one, kicking inside her. Or did he have a way of knowing that only old folks of the North have? "Tell Grandfather I'll send him some cigarettes. He needs—"

Suddenly, a terrible image made her drop the pencil. She saw Jimmy lying in the snow, bleeding to death, and "Mike," smelling the blood, looking at him with the wolf in his eyes. Impulsively, she rose and ran up the stairs to go call the police to look for him. Her hand was on the knob when she heard the familiar scratching noise.

But this time it was so loud and rapid, she could almost

feel the claws on her flesh. A miserable whine penetrated the door.

A voice outside, sounding near yet far, far away yelled, "There he is! He's the one!"

She heard three rapid shots and a muffled thrashing of furred flesh and bones against the door. The leaden nose of a bullet lodged in the door stared at her as she sank to her knees in a daze.

Jimmy had often seen the old, rotten caboose. The sight of it caused a faint tremor of fear. Even so, now for the first time, he went inside.

He wanted to be alone in a small, dark place. But a shaft of cold, gray light fell through a small window. He sank to his knees on the damp, ripped mattress and lay on his side, his knees pulled up against his chest, his hands crossed under his throat, huddled on the spot where the tube of light struck. The mattress had an intense smell of old urine and the dust of many summers. Lying there, feeling the throbbing pain in the palm of his hand, he was afraid, but felt unable to move.

He recalled only vaguely the image of his mother's angry face, of the silver scissors hurling across the room toward him. The sight of the drying blood seemed a final expression of everything. He was not sorry about the wound his mother had inflicted. The pain and the blood made him feel closer to her than her usual silence, her deafness to him, her avoiding eyes ever did. But he regretted throwing that dirty chunk of frozen snow at "Mike" and calling him a bastard. Recalling lucidly the mark of red that rose on the side of the dog's head, he wept.

He was scarcely aware of his *own* hunger. A greater

emptiness ached inside him. But he felt *"Mike's"* hunger keenly. He had failed to feed him. Shivering with fear and remorse and the cold that penetrated the caboose, he yearned to feel the huge, furry animal warmth of "Mike."

After a while, his nerves began slowly to calm and he thought of other things. He saw the broadness of Walt's back, those times before he began staying every night and his mother would order Jimmy to go out and play. (With whom? The children of the soldiers who were born in the states, who called him an Eskimo and chased him suddenly in the middle of a game?) He would go for a long walk and come back in the dark and knock timidly with his almost-frozen fist on the door. Sometimes Walt opened it and Jimmy hesitated to descend into the basement house. Or he would sit on a cinder block and stare into the warm, bright rooms of Louise's house and watch her and her husband eat supper, or watch her give the baby a bath. He somehow didn't like the baby, but it reminded him of a vague time when he was happy and safe, in another home.

He wondered if Louise knew that he loved her. She didn't love him, or she would understand why he couldn't chain up "Mike" during the day with the other dogs that pulled his sled when he delivered papers. It was bad enough at night, lying awake, listening to "Mike" whine to be released. He didn't care if the other dogs weren't free, because he loved only "Mike." Walking with him in the boondocks, he was always aware of "Mike's" freedom and envied him, but tried to share his freedom, and sometimes did, running, running, running.

But he didn't want to think about anything. Looking around, he became aware that the caboose was filled chaotically with abandoned objects. Something red stuck out from under the mattress like a tongue. Uncurling his legs and arms, he reached out and pulled at the soft piece of cloth. He held a pair of red panties up to the shaft of light. It had a musty smell that strangely soothed him. A name, stitched across the red silky material, startled, bewildered him: MIKE. A jet flew over the caboose, causing it to shudder.

He got up and began groping about in the shadows, feeling strange forms. As he examined each object in the light, he felt as though he were discovering familiar trail marks that would lead him from lost to home. A nine-year-old calendar with mildewed numbers under a picture of Christ, standing with his hands tied before a king who was pointing his finger at him; a corroded pair of wings; a rusty coffee pot; a baby's knitted bootie; a moldy combat boot; a blue organdy dress with a rip down the front; a baby's shirt, food stains frozen into the fabric; rusty hairpins; a woman's old shoes; a child's picture book in shreds; a rotten bottle nipple.

Then he found some letters, scattered over the sagging floor. They were written by Belle to her family, only a few of them signed, none of them mailed. "Dear Momma" or "Dear Grandfather," and all about Mike and little Jimmy and being so happy. Looking at the faded pictures made his heart throb worse than the palm of his hand. Blurred, brown images of a tall, stout man in an Air Force uniform, smiling, hugging a young, black-haired girl in a thin dress, who looked up at him, smiling; the image of a little, wrinkled old man with snow-white hair and slit eyes, smoking a pipe, a dark look of irritation and disapproval stamped on his face; the image of a woman resembling him, sitting in front of a black shack with snow on the roof and nets hanging in the side yard.

Jimmy felt very weak. In his mind an image of this house that he had lost and found loomed bright and warm, but the darkness he saw and the coldness he felt around him in the caboose, penetrated and dissolved the image. He sank to his knees on the mattress again. The light was fading now. He drew his knees up against his chest and crossed his arms beneath his throat, the soft red silk in his wounded hand. He was very weary, so weary that at first the sound of the jet was very faint and the familiar longing rose up in him only vaguely, the longing to grow up quickly and join the Air Force and fly a jet and go faster than sound and climb higher than the mountains, and be free. And he fell asleep before the sound of the jet grew suddenly, briefly louder, and woke him.

Louise took a bite of the cookie and knelt to the floor of the bright kitchen to place it in Bobby's mouth. But Bobby was hugging his white teddy bear, whispering secrets into its chewed ear. When he saw the cookie, he licked it tentatively, looking up at Louise before he bit into it.

She was hurriedly baking a cake for Sunday dinner, trying to have it on the table when John arrived. Because some captain was going to fly to Seattle to spend Easter evening with his family, John had to leave his own family to service the jet.

The oven made the kitchen so hot that she had to open the door to let some air in. But it was too cold for Bobby, so she set him and his teddy bear behind the door.

As she hovered contentedly over the steaming pots, she imagined what it would be like when John's hitch was up, and she and he and Bobby would return to the Bronx and she would be cooking for him there, waiting for him to come home from the butcher shop he yearned to own. It still seemed a little strange being only an Alaskan wife, with all the things that were home missing. But she was happy. The mountains were beautiful and the cold wasn't damp. But the neighbors were far from desirable.

She knew all about Belle from Grace, who lived on the other side. She didn't mind talking to Grace. At least *her* home was not a *hole*. That rotten old-fashioned little caboose Grace told her about had been worse. Then, too, she had had a lover—an Air Force man like her own husband. The soldier she had now probably wouldn't stay long. The more Belle's stomach swelled, the more restless he would become.

It was bad for the boy, though. Twelve years old, and he had never had a real mother's care. What a shy, sweet, moody child. She regretted being cross with him, because she liked him. Once, when she saw him standing in the yard throwing a stick for "Mike" to retrieve until the dog was worn out with running, she felt the impulse to call the boy to her and hug him.

But that dog. She did not like "Mike," though she didn't hate him either. It was a beautiful white dog, but when she passed it and Jimmy on the road, she felt a faint spasm of panic.

The television set in the living room was too loud. She went in and turned it down. Through the front window, she could see the light in the tower of the Lighthouse Methodist Church. Even if it *was* Easter, she would not harass John into going to services. They would watch an Easter program on TV and eat popcorn and maybe even get into another popcorn-throwing fight.

She watched the reverend and his son go into the church to prepare for the service.

She remembered the night three summers ago when the reverend asked if anyone wanted to give his heart to Jesus. She knew John was embarrassed, but she rose anyway, and, with Bobby unborn in her stomach, she walked down the aisle. Jimmy's mother had forced him to come—alone, as usual. His head was turned toward her, watching her come toward him. She was moved by the tender, entreating look in his eyes as he slowly rose to his feet. Not until she had passed him did she have the feeling that he had wanted her to take his hand and lead him to the altar.

She was walking back toward the kitchen when a muffled scream from outside startled her. Her heart stopped, and for a moment she stood rigidly still. But then she recognized the roar of a jet as a faint tremor passed through the walls of the house. The pot was boiling over, so she did not have a chance to glance at the space behind the door to see it occupied only by the teddy bear, its glass eyes touching the floor.

Through a crack between the open door and the frame, Bobby saw the dog.

He had seen it before, but it had not seen him. He had called to it, but like Momma or Daddy sometimes, it had not understood. But he knew that its fur would be warm and sweet-smelling, like Teddy's, only it was much bigger, almost as big as Momma, and she was a good softness. He let the teddy bear fall from his embrace, and, stepping on its hand, he walked out the door on his unsteady legs into the cold air and onto the snow. He had almost expected Momma to catch him up suddenly from behind, and, scolding, carry him back into the warm room.

The beautiful dog was white as the deep snow, snow so deep Bobby couldn't walk far out in it. The dog wasn't walking steadily either. It limped like Daddy when he acted funny in the living room. He thought the dog saw him, and he wanted it to come over to him so he could hug it. But it walked past him. Then he saw the red spot on the side of its head. Poor doggy. It hurt like the men in the TV.

Bobby called to the dog. It stopped, one foot poised above the snow, and turned, and its pretty eyes looked at him. This time it understood. Bobby was getting cold. As the dog came toward him, walking in a funny stiff way, its head down, its eyes looking up at him, Bobby anticipated feeling the warm, white fur when he would hug it.

When it was close enough, Bobby reached out his hand and touched its fur. The hair was like needles of ice, so cold it nearly burned. He was suddenly drowned in a tremendous noise. Then he saw the lip curl and the white fang flash.

The Pale Horse of Fear

*I*N the autumn dusk the ridges on the horizon were
softly contrasting tones of lavender, and as wind-
strummed trees moved in the evening mist, grass by the
road shimmered, and two brothers walked a short distance
apart along the dirt road. Bains walked with a dragging
limp: a wiggly scar followed him down the weed-ragged
road. His arms encircled a worn wicker basket heaped
with persimmons, his knotted fingers stained with juice.
When Bains's awkward gait dislodged a persimmon, Robbie's shadow disappeared into Bains's as the child stooped
to pick up the fallen fruit. Smiling, he polished the persimmon in the whirling abundance of his golden hair
where a few dead leaves were stuck. "It's bitter!"

Bains glanced over his shoulder at the graceful boy in
the pink sunsuit. His vivid lips writhed, turned the pallor
of his teats. Looking ahead at the light glowing through
the trees from the kitchen of their house, Bains said, "The
bitter ones'll draw your mouth up so you can't open it,
and you can't breathe, and you smother to death." The
wind tumbled his thin brown hair down over his eyes.

"Aw . . ." Robbie spit out the bitter mush and, shriek-
ing out of mock terror, began to run, zigzagging over the
soft dirt road, trying to outrun his shadow.

Bains deliberately inhaled the mild rawness of the air.
"Gonna rain," he said to himself.

Robbie stopped running and skipped beside his big

brother. "Bains," he said, between gasps for breath, "Why can't—nobody—run faster—than their—shadow?" His voice was thin, distant, as though the wind carried it from deep out of the woods, where the persimmon trees stood.

"I don't know."

"Does Momma know?"

"I don't reckon."

"I bet Daddy knows. *He* knows ever'thing."

"Daddy's dead."

"I bet Daddy's my shadow."

"Sometimes your shadow is behind you, following you, and sometimes it gets bigger than you are."

"How come, Bains?"

"Well, I don't know. But when Daddy was in his coffin in the living room, Momma sat beside him all night, with just a candle, rocking back and forth in the rocking chair Gran'maw give us. And her shadow was on the wall, and it moved ever'time she did, ten times bigger than her. Her stomach was great big. And two weeks later *you* was borned."

"Did Daddy have a shadow, too, that night, Bains?"

"No. He was dead . . . and white as the moon."

Robbie ran up the red clay bank and climbed up on the first rung of the old, sagging wooden fence, in the summer draped with honeysuckle.

White as Moonlight? White as *he* is, Bains?" Robbie's voice rose and tumbled on the wind.

Bains stopped, the basket of persimmons heavy in his arms. Robbie was pointing at Moonlight, the clumsy old stallion that all year, every year, since Daddy died, remained in the abandoned meadow, grazing. During all the seasons, the grass was green. A small, weather-beaten shed, gaping here and there from the loss of several boards, stood under a lone oak, almost leaning against it. Bains remembered looking often through the bedroom window with Robbie, talking about the strange way the tree blotted out the moon, its glow like luminous cobwebs in the leaves, and the dim white bulk of the horse moving in the moonlit shed.

"Was Daddy white as Moonlight?"

"Come on, Robbie. Momma's home. She'll be worried."

"He looks so lonesome!" yelled Robbie, sliding down the bank on his rump.

"You're gonna get your sunsuit dirty, Robbie."

"Gimme a 'simmon."

"You'll get sick. It's suppertime, anyhow."

Grasping the loose hanging tail of Bains's faded blue shirt, Robbie swung his other arm like the pendulum of a grandfather clock as they walked down the soft dirt road. "Mooooon—light—is the—loooone—sommmest—perrrr—son in the whole, whole, whole, big-o world!"

"He ain't no person. He's a big, lazy horse that can hardly walk. And someday the lightnin's gonna burn him up like a piece of burnt bacon."

"No, it ain't, nezer! Bains, don't talk so scary, will you not?"

"Ut, oh, a drop-a rain."

"Whur?"

"On that persimmon. I could feel it coming in my foot."

"Wish I could feel rain inside my foot. . . . Hey, Bains, let's us play with Moonlight tamar'. We ain't never played with him in our whole, whole life."

"I used to, 'fore he got so old. He's old as me. We was born the same night. Midnight—when the whole world was asleep. And the woods caught afire."

"Is that how come they's old black trees whur we play?"

"Yeah, that's why."

"Moonlight's all alone, but *you* got *me*, Bains."

As they rounded the bend of the road, over which hung the limbs of a white, tan-patched sycamore, Bains saw a big, red, stream-lined car parked in front of their house. They reached the front porch just as a trembling curtain of rain swept toward them over the ridge. Walking through the twilight rooms, they heard laughter. A man sat in the kitchen with Momma.

"Here's your Uncle Emmett come to see us," Momma said, wiping tears of laughter from her eyes. She had not really laughed in a long time. She was always so silent, so tired when she came home from work at the knitting mill in town. And her feet scraped over the linoleum as she moved about the kitchen preparing supper for her "two wild flowers." And while she sat in the rocking chair in the late evening, asleep, her head back, her mouth slightly open, Robbie would sit on her lap and pick the lint from her hair. They stood there, Bains with the basket of persimmons in his arms, Robbie, mouth open, hands on his head, awesomely enjoying their mother's rare laughter.

To Bains, Uncle Emmett was a gray memory. At his father's funeral six years ago, he had worn a yellow straw hat with a red band. When he took it off, his bald head had looked pure white, but now it was as pink as Robbie's sunsuit.

To Robbie, Uncle Emmett was an exciting stranger, who promised that after supper he would show them the brand new pairs of shoes he had in a big suitcase in his car, which he called his "buggy."

After supper, Uncle Emmett sat cross-legged, tapping ashes from his stubby cigar into his cracked coffee cup. The aroma of coffee was wonderful and somewhat strange to Bains, for since his daddy died it had been absent from the kitchen. Uncle Emmett's voice was so loud and deep in the large kitchen it nearly drowned out the murmur of rain on the roof, the rattle of window glass in their frames, and the light of the kerosene lamp in the middle of the table made his bald head shine, as he talked of old times. "You were just a dishrag in heaven then, Goldenrod," he said to Robbie, stirring his blunt fingers in Robbie's swirling blond hair. And he talked of Moonlight. His name had been Snow, but no one had called him that for years, and recently Robbie had renamed him.

As Uncle Emmett talked of Moonlight, calling him Snow, speaking vividly of him as he had been years ago, Bains, fascinated, stared out the window. Faint signs of movement flickered between the cracks and the gaps in the shed. Moonlight was probably wet, skin to bone, standing in mud that made a sucking sound when he lifted his hoof. Bains suddenly remembered a faint fear he had had of the horse when he was little, and it seemed odd now that until Robbie and Uncle Emmett started talking about him, it had been a long time since he had really been aware of the stallion's existence—it had always just been there, like the moon or the sun.

"And remember, Emma, the state fair, when Samp won first prize with Snow? It was kinda beautiful how proud Samp was. Remember?"

Momma nodded slowly, a faint smile puffing her sunken cheeks.

"What ever become of that gorgeous horse?"

"His name's Moonlight, Uncle Emmett," said Robbie,

running around the table, striking a knife and a fork together. "The rain's raining all over him down in the meadow." Uncle Emmett caught Robbie and hoisted him up on his lap.

"So he's still alive."

Momma nodded, pressing her blue-veined fists against her temples. "Robbie, please don't bang things. Momma's worn out."

"Moonlight is the saddest horse in the world, and the whole, big-o sky, Uncle Emmett."

"You know, Emma, it's a wonder when that horse stepped on Bains's foot that Samp didn't . . . ." Uncle Emmett's voice died away when he saw Momma's hand stiffen and a startled look shine in her eyes.

Shocked, Bains, trembling, stared at his mother.

She feebly put her hand out to Bains.

"You've never even told him, Emma?" Bains's mother shook her head. "I'm awful sorry, Emma. Dad-*burn*, I'm sorry."

Bains's face was contorted as if he were crying, but no tears came, only an aching hard lump in his throat, and his heart fluttered like a terrified moth beating its dusty wings against a bright light bulb.

"What's the matter?" squealed Robbie, bouncing of his own accord on Uncle Emmett's knee, looking at the odd, silent faces. "Ever'body laugh!" Ever'body laugh!" Striking the edge of the table with the knife in uneven tempo, he forced high, shrill laughter.

Bains rose abruptly, knocking over his chair with a backward thrust of his lame foot, and struck Robbie across the mouth. "Quit it! Quit it!"

"Bains, he's little!" Momma screamed.

Uncle Emmett's face turned red, and he looked awkwardly out the window. Robbie, motionless as stone on his Uncle's lap, his mouth swelling from the blow, stared in terrified wonder at Bains.

Uplifted, Bains's hand trembled in the glare of the hanging light bulb. *It was kinda beautiful how proud Samp was. Remember?*

Momma stood behind him, one thin hand around his waist, the other gently patting his cheek, Robbie's sudden scream ringing in Bains's hot ears. A burning tear fell on the nape of his neck as he struggled to loose himself from Momma's weeping consoling caress.

"I'm sorry, Emma. Dad-burnit to hell, I'm sorry," Uncle Emmett muttered over and over, shaking his shining head.

Bains limped out of the room, stumbled through the darkness of the other rooms until he came to the closed door of his bedroom. It was stuck. He had to twist the knob violently and jar the damp, swollen wood with his narrow shoulders to get it to swing in, knocking the knee of his lame leg against the frame. He fell across the damp mattress. Rain coming through the open window soaked his shirt. He lay there, his mouth open on the moist sheet, staring at the rain-sparkled window sill. The ache pulsing in his throat, the emptiness in his belly made him feel too swollen for the size of the room.

He awakened to the sound of a door opening. Light glowed on the wall, and through a film of stinging sleep-acid, he saw two shadows. The door closed, pulling the light out. Bare feet moved toward the bed slowly upon the wet floor. The mattress sagged, the springs sighed, Bains heard broken breathing, then felt cool, moist lips on the nape of his neck. "I love you, Bains," Robbie said, as though breathed instead of spoken, as though the wind had carried a murmur of rain from deep in the woods where the persimmon trees stood.

A cold hand on his damp shoulders awakened Bains. Mist-like moonlight made Momma's pale face a blurred form in the darkness. Her dry lips were pale purple. "Time to get up, honey." Momma wore her starched green uniform. Behind her temples her hair was smooth, a fuzzy bun on her nape. She left the door ajar, and her faint footsteps echoed on the dark air until the only sound was the movement of rusty springs as Bains got out of bed.

Standing by the bed in the clammy clothes in which he had fallen asleep, he watched the faint movements of his sleeping brother's body under the faded quilt. The golden hair glowed softly in the dim room. A rooster's cry sounded somewhere in the hollow as Bains bent to kiss his brother's closed eyes.

Frost covered the red car, blinding its windows. Momma leaned against the fender, waiting for the factory bus to appear around the bend in the road, her fingers nervously fumbling with her hair.

Bains reached up into the leaves of the maple tree and pulled his damp paper satchel down from a limb.

"Where's Robbie, honey?"

Bains heard the rattling of the bus on the other side of the hill. "Sleep. . . . Don't feel like having him help me."

"Bains . . ."

"Yes'um?"

"Promise Momma you'll forget about last night."

Bains looked away, toward the mist-shrouded mountains. Through the trees he saw Moonlight standing like an ivory statue in the tall grass. Shrugging his shoulders, he walked down the road toward town. A red glow suddenly splashed the gray sky. In his mind, he saw red, sleep-heavy men heaving shovels of coal into the furnaces of the foundry by the river in the heart of the town. The bus rattled past him, rocking upon its axles like a small boat, and through one of the frosty windows he saw Momma's face.

In the thick shadow of a gray stone church, he bent over his satchel, stuffing it with the morning papers. In a sleep-numbed alcove of his mind, he swung an ax into the brain of the white stallion, and blood, cold as ice water, trickled down his arms, lifted to strike again.

At the end of his route, he stopped as usual at the railroad station for a cup of hot chocolate. Exhausted, he fell asleep before the steam had stopped rising from the cup.

Robbie was shaking his arm. Bains's eyes opened upon Momma's faded jade coat, hanging from Robbie's head like a tent.

Drinking chocolate, the brothers talked. When the great trains roared by, steam and rain hit the soot-grimed window panes and rolled into the station through the open doorway.

"Uncle Emmett left his suitcase, Bains. They's a million trillion shoes in it. You can wear the orange ones. Bains, what you thinking about so hard? Quit staring at nothing, Bains. You'll put your eyes out. Let's go home and get you dry. Your clothes so wet it looks like blue skin. Quit staring at the rain. You can wear the orange ones, Bains." Inside the hooded shadow of the jade coat, Robbie's eyes pleaded.

Finally, Bains stood up and allowed Robbie to lead him home along the railroad tracks, through the wet fields under the dripping trees, down the muddy road beside the meadow. Robbie pulled at the empty satchel hanging from Bains's shoulder, playing like it was a bell-tower rope. "Dong, dong, dong."

All day rain fell upon the dim house, mist hovered at the windows. The brothers spoke in whispers as they handled the new, raw smelling leather. They tried on all sizes. The squeaking of leather, the clumsy clop-clop-clopping of footsteps, charging aimlessly through the rooms, down the steps to the cool cellar and up to the hot attic, echoed along the silent, sagging walls. Robbie polished the old-fashioned orange shoes with an orange peel, squealing with delight at the increasing luster. With shy pride, Bains wore the glowing shoes all day long.

Through a circle he had drawn on the misty pane, Bains stared listlessly toward the pasture and at the pale ivory form standing in a stupor in the rain. *It was kinda beautiful how proud Samp was. Remember?* Begging to play hide-and-go-seek, volunteering to be It, Robbie pulled Bains away from the window.

All around Bains where he hid in the solid, clammy blackness of the cellar were shelves of fruit preserves, linked by networks of spider webs that stuck to his face. When he was as little as Robbie, he had accidentally locked himself in the cellar. Daddy had been far off in the fields and Momma had gone into town, and for a long time Bains had groped wildly in the murky dampness, screaming for his Daddy until his throat felt raw, bruising his face against the fruit jars, terrified by thoughts of the shapeless ghosts in the tales Daddy had told on dark winter nights, his feet on the fender of the heater.

Clop, clop, clop, clop, slowly descending, rang bluntly in his ears. "Quit it!" Bains cried out. "Don't walk that way! Robbie! Robbie! Stop it! Please, I'm telling you to quit it!" In the numb silence, Bains's heart pounded like blood in his ears. Then the clop . . . clop . . . clop . . . began again, heavily, more slowly. He could not see his brother. *Was* it his brother? "Robbie! I'm scared! Is that you, Robbie? Who is it? I'll kill you!" Stepping back blindly into the murkiness, stumbling over baskets and dusty fruit jars, Bains screamed until the sound ached inside his head.

"One, two, three on Bains!" screamed Robbie. Then the loud clopping rapidly ascended the stairs. The door opened harshly, and Robbie's voice echoed shrilly down the passage. "You're It, Bains!"

That night, Momma burned the fish, but she trimmed it, and they left only white bones on their plates.

"Momma, you know what Kester Styles told me?"

"Robbie, honey, how did you get all that mud on your sunsuit?"

"In the meadow. The mud's deep as quicksand, Momma. I squashed-squashed in it all the way to the shed."

Bains looked up from his plate and stared across the table at Robbie. "What did you go to the shed for?"

"To play with Moonlight."

"You stay away from that old horse."

"Why, Bains?"

"Robbie . . ."

"Uh? Ma'am?"

"You feed the chickens?"

"Yes'um. Momma, you know what Kester Styles told me today?"

"No, what, Honey? Bains, your Uncle Emmett was by here this evening while you all was crackin' walnuts down by the springhouse. Bains, I told you not to wear those shoes!"

"They purdy, Momma," said Robbie. "Bains an' me

shined 'um up so nice and purdy. I unlaced 'um for 'im when they hurt his foot."

"Uncle Emmett was mad as thunder, Bains. Said he couldn't sell 'em now. All worn and out of shape. So he left the orange ones for you."

"Oh, goody, Bains. I love those ol' orange shoes, don't you, Bains?"

"Yeah."

"I bet they even let you be buried in 'um. Bains, you know what Kester told me down at the store while ago?"

"What, Robbie?"

"Said his Uncle Hobe once't had this ol' mule that went plumb crazy."

"That's nothin'."

"Now, Bains. Let Robbie tell about it."

"But, Bains, this ol' mule went crazy just walkin' 'round in a circle. Just kep' on goin' 'round an' 'round an' 'round for a million years, and one day it plopped dead. I don't believe it though 'cause Kester lies something awful."

Bains stood up.

"What you gettin' up for, Honey? Bains, come back to the table. You ain't had your persimmon preserves yet."

"I'll go get 'im, Momma."

"No, Robbie . . . sit down. He's gone down to the meadow."

"Oh, he's gonna play with Moonlight. Momma, make him take me with him."

"Eat your persimmon preserves, Honey. Bains'll be back d'reckly. He's just standing at the edge of the meadow."

An hour before the time he was accustomed to getting

up, Bains opened his eyes. Thick frost covered the windowpane. Tenderly, as though unveiling a statue, Bains pulled down the quilt that was over Robbie's face, disturbed to see his face covered. He dressed quietly, and, to avoid passing Momma's room, he left the house by the back door.

Wading in the grass, he walked around the house to the maple tree and pulled down his damp satchel. Then he climbed over the broken fence. Walking through the tall grass in the meadow, he heard a dull thud from the leaning shed. He stopped, and suddenly began to breathe very quickly.

Standing in the lopsided doorway of the shed, Bains had a sudden impulse to flog the horse with his satchel, excite such wild terror that it would smash its own brains to a pulp against the weathered boards.

But excited by his desire to carry out the scheme, he merely looped the satchel around the neck of the submissive animal. As Bains led Moonlight away from the black shed and out into the open meadow, he was only vaguely conscious that the horse was behind him, that its name was Snow or Moonlight, or even that it was a horse. The only thing he was aware of was the intense feeling in his stomach that made him conscious of the greatness of his power.

For an hour, he led the bulky, plodding horse round and round and round in a wide circle. When he heard the pale echo of the front door closing in the mauve darkness, he lay flat on the ground, the tall grass bending over him, until the ugly green bus passed noisily by. Then Bains got up, dew on his hair, and went on to pick up his papers near the railroad station just as the five A. M. express came roaring through the trees.

Every morning until the first of spring, Bains rose, the acid of sleep in his eyes, and went out to the shed. Moonlight was always standing in a bulky, nodding stupor, striking blunt wood-music in his sleep. And he led the pale horse out to the same spot and went through the monotonous routine, a merry-go-round with one pale horse and a walking rider. Toward the end of this time, which seemed after a while to be a part of Bains's nocturnal dreams, unrelated to his daylight life, the animal began to plod in the circle, the always diminishing circle, without Bains's guidance. One morning Bains went to the shed and, finding it empty, saw the horse standing ready in the open field.

Having kept a meaningless dawn vigil over him, Bains left Moonlight plodding in his worn circle. Later, listlessly pitching rolled newspapers upon dark, damp porches, listening to the series of dull plunks as they fell, Bains became a sluggish dream figure in his own memory of Robbie and red clover. One evening last summer, supper was steaming on the table in the dusk-lit kitchen, and Robbie was nowhere to be found. The echo "Robbieeeeeeeeee, Rob-bieeeeeeee" had trembled in the hollow as Bains searched every secret niche. Supper had gotten cold on the table. Bains did not find Robbie until late that evening when moonlight glowed on the table where Momma sat, her fingers trembling over her eyes, her breath coming in soft rasping sighs. Behind the chicken house, worm-riddled and soft with rot, he had found Robbie asleep, submerged in a heap of red clover, soft with moonglow. For a moment, he appeared dead. Wisps of Robbie's golden hair showed among the clover, his slender arm lay across his brow, and now and then lobes of clover moved at the twitching of Robbie's pink fingers. Under the clover, his breath moved like waves of silence. Bains stared down in confused wonder at his brother, and as the scene assumed a hue both grotesque and melancholy, he felt that the strange restlessness beginning in his heart would never leave him. To avoid waking Robbie, Bains had gently lifted him and carried him into the house, the amber clover dripping from his hair, through the kitchen, down the dark hallway and into the bedroom, where he laid him in the cold moon-reflection on their bed. Lying beside Robbie, Bains had inhaled the mellow aroma of the clover that still clung to Robbie's hair and clothes. Finally, his blinking eyes had closed in a tight, silver cocoon of sleep.

All during the winter Bains forbade Robbie to go with him on the route, leaving the dark room of breathing silence with very delicate footsteps. One morning, from far out in the meadow, Bains thought he saw the pale face of his brother beyond the windowpane. And that night in bed, Robbie said, "Bains, I woke up last night and I thought I saw Moonlight walking around in a circle in the moonlight."

When summer came, the heat was constantly thick and heavy, and little rain fell. The grass in the meadow was long and thick, full of insects with loud voices that together sent up into the humid air a dull electric drone. But in the center of the meadow, a circular clearing lay like a brown fuzzy eye staring up into the glaring sun. And constantly the huge horse tranquilly lunged round and round, now and then dipping his coarse, matted head to the dry stubble, licking it into his mouth with his hot tongue.

Flesh disappeared from his body little by little, shrinking in upon his languid bones. The brook beneath the trees went dry, the bed became a crust of cracked clay, and small stones glared in the sun. No one could say whether the horse would have gone there to drink even if there had been water, for he did not cease to drag his shadow around the circle in the morning and follow it in the evening. Through the night he plodded on, nodding his head, heavy with the clabbered smoke of fatigue, until finally his legs gave beneath him like soft gray putty, and he lay, a quivering heap, haven for the fleas of the night. And if Robbie had not come to him through the swirling sea of grass to the barren circle in the humid midnight with a tipping pail of water, the horse would surely have died.

The circle was almost a perfect one, and in his mind-less revolutions, he was, day by day, moving in from the periphery toward the center, leaving trampled dead grass in his sluggish wake, while outside the circle, tall weeds and wild flowers bent under the hot winds.

Boys passing from the small factory town nearby saw this clearing, and before long Bains acquired many friends who came to his yard nearly every day carrying gloves, balls, and bats, who, smiling, set out with him, trampling the mellow flowers to the clearing, where they played ball until darkness fell and fireflies glowed.

With little thought of his foot now, Bains developed a new hatred for the horse because he was always in the way, spoiling the game.

Bains was very happy with his new friends. They even allowed him to run the bases after striking the ball into the sky. In the late evening, as he lay beside Robbie in bed, thinking of the events of the day, he was filled with a peace that was sublimely difficult to bear.

Before they could play, the boys had to make a clam-

orous fuss to frighten Moonlight away from the circle. At
first when the boys began slapping the horse's fly-speckled
rump with their gloves, spitting into his face, screaming
at him until their throats got raw, Bains felt a perplexing
resentment. But after a while he joined the gang in terri-
fying the horse, and the irritating bewilderment faded
away.

The game was hardly under way before the animal suddenly became an obstacle. A boy would run into him
without the faintest premonition that he was standing
there. Time and again, they drove him from his circle,
bombarding him with noisy abuse, while Robbie, who
wasn't allowed to join in the game, jumped up and down,
jarring burning tears from his eyes. Forced away, Moonlight would stand staring into the sun, his eyes swollen
with animal bewilderment.

One day, even before they had reached the clearing,
the heat had made the boys very moody. They came silently into the meadow, carrying things that had become
their weapons against Moonlight as well as their play-
things, Bains hobbling among them, Robbie quietly following. The horse was ponderously tracing the infinity
of his circle. By then, it was routine to begin immediately,
without words, to chase the animal away. But he was
very stubborn. The gloves made heavy thuds on his body,
but he did not break his stride. Within the larger circle,
the remaining circle of grass was very small, and the
horse seemed to twist in upon himself. Again and again,
the boys struck the horse, threw hot grass and sharp rocks
into his face. Then one of them struck his head with a
bat.

For the first time, he whinnied and slobbered. The
other boys with bats moved in and swung. And then sud-

denly the horse bolted and ran crazily, zigzagging into the black woods.

After the boys had gone, Robbie stayed, lying outside the circle under a canopy of dead grass, waiting for Moonlight to return. Just before dusk, he heard a sound in the grass, felt a slight tremor in the ground under him. He raised his bright head and looked around. Moonlight was in his circle again, as if nothing had happened. But as Robbie walked toward him, he saw green saliva hanging from his teeth. He was walking more slowly than ever before, hardly able to revolve around the circle, as Robbie, his hand extended, approached him.

Bains found Robbie in a bed of trampled, twisted grass that had specks of blood in it. Robbie's hair was matted with dried blood, his face was crushed, his broken chest heaved with feeble breath. With an unbearable ache in his throat, Bains carried Robbie across the meadow past the shadowy shed, through the tall, motionless grass to the house. As he walked, he seemed to feel the red eyes watching him from the somber woods.

When Momma saw her child dangling like a broken doll in the arms of the cripple, she did not speak. She simply took the boy with swift tenderness into her own arms and carried him through the hot, dim hallway to his room. She shut the door, leaving Bains alone in the hall.

Bains ran into town and told the doctor that his little brother had been stomped to death by a mad horse. Coming back through the street, he told everyone that the mad horse was in the burnt woods. They went home for their guns.

Bains did not go back into the house. He felt that he could never again look into Momma's face. He pulled down the wicker basket from the wall of the coal house and went across the road to the hillside of clover. He did not look at the No Trespassing sign. The moon shone as he filled the basket with clover bells.

As he started down the hill with his arms full of the basket, someone shouted to him from the shrouded darkness of the trees. At first he thought it was the horse, but then it shouted again, louder. Running down the hill, Bains snagged his lame foot in a gopher hole and sprawled face forward upon the ground. When he got up again, all the clover was spread out on the grass, and the basket was empty.

Bains moved through the hallway, dragging his foot behind him. A single clover bell fell from his hair into his hand and this he laid in his brother's cold, rigid, open palm.

Through the window, he saw the torches of the angry townsmen moving in the burnt woods. He did not speak to his mother, who sat in the shadows, but kissed his brother's broken face, and went out into the yard. Momma's voice came from the dark porch, from behind the black screen. "When morning comes, all three of you will be dead. It won't matter if no one picks the lint from my hair."

Momma's words meant nothing to Bains. He hobbled away from the porch and toward the woods, where torch lights loomed among the trees like sun-blasted cobwebs, and distorted echoes of anger rose on the hot night air. The moon was so full and bright it was easy to avoid the many little holes and gullies in the meadow.

Just as Bains came to the edge of the woods, he saw an illumination that came from deep inside. He knew that a torch held too high had set the woods on fire, but he limped on, deeper and deeper into the woods toward the distant light, aware of men among the trees around him as they ran away from the fire. He hoped the beast was looking for him also.

God Proud

*I*N the Cove, the mild air had slushed the snow. At the curve, where Frank expected a dip and then the ford, he slammed on the brakes. An earthmover blocked the road. The stream that crossed the road gurgled around its traction belts, and melting snow streaked the back windows. He had expected peace to begin at the stream, but as he edged his motorcycle around the gigantic orange bulldozer, hate made Frank shudder.

In front of it, about to start up again, he saw the other machines, orange in the early light, parked at odd angles, in and along the road. He rode through puddles where they'd gouged up holes, the water splashing up under his corduroys and into his boots. A raw pain throbbed in his throat as he passed the machines, afraid he'd look between two of them and see Gran'paw's house and everything around it in ruins, as though Indian marauders had attacked.

But curving between familiar elms, he saw the white posts on the porch standing out cold and serene from the front of the house, one window catching the slant of light straining through the clouds.

In the same moment, he saw the construction shack. A red and white sign: J. BEAZLEY CONTRACTORS. Glad to see a name, somebody personal to curse, he called the bastard every kind of sonofabitch he could think of.

When he stopped at the gate, he saw Gran'paw sitting

in the window. A light lace of snow dripped off the sharp edge of the tin roof, and behind the bead drape the dripping made was the parlor window where Gran'paw sat behind the net curtains. By the way his shoulders bowed forward and his arms hung, Frank guessed that he had a shotgun in his lap.

He didn't know what he expected instead, but it startled him to think that that was what Gran'paw intended. Stepping onto the porch, Frank glimpsed the glassy cast of Gran'paw's eyes and supposed he'd kept watch all night.

He knocked, knowing that the door would be locked. Frank heard Gran'paw's chair scrape as he got up, and the butt of his shotgun struck the wall as he came to the door.

Without speaking, he gave Frank a nod and a little lift of his hand as it came away from the knob. Frank knocked the heels of his boots together, scuffed back the snow, and before he could step over the sill, the dogs were all over him. He danced around and around the porch with them and into the house, Gran'paw speaking softly but sternly to them, looking Frank over, up and down, trying to catch the look in his eyes.

On the way back to the parlor where he could see the road better, Gran'paw motioned Frank to bring a chair from beside the fireplace. Frank dragged a cane-bottom chair behind him and tried to pat down the dogs with the other hand. He sat beside the window opposite Gran'paw, watching him get the dogs settled down on the rag rug, and when he looked for Frank's eyes, Frank was looking right into his. Gran'paw saw instantly that Frank was bluffing, so he looked through the curtains.

They didn't talk. Frank looked at the dogs, sitting still, as they'd been told, but nervous, suddenly opening and closing their mouths, twitching their ears. A little sound in the wood as it settled from Frank coming in, and they would jerk up their heads and look at Frank and Gran'-paw. The lace end of the curtain on Frank's side had gotten looped over his leg. Gran'paw was glancing at him. Light was growing brighter in the yard.

"Want me to whip up something to eat?" Frank asked.

"I ain't hungry."

Frank waited a while, stroking the curtain, reminded of the feel of summer screens. "How long has it been started?"

Gran'paw didn't move. The light got clearer on his face. "You goin' back?"

"No."

"Never?"

"No, sir."

Getting up, he laid the shotgun across Frank's lap as though it were a stick of wood and went somewhere in the back of the house.

He came back with a rifle and a pack of cartridges that he put on the sill where the curtain parted, and, with one motion, he sat down and placed the rifle across his knees.

Frank felt the shotgun heavy on his legs.

He thought of the letter from the draft board in his jacket pocket ordering him to report for induction, and still vivid in his mind was the image of his father aiming a shotgun at him. He had anticipated that moment so long, and so intensely, that he felt now that he had almost willed it, that his father had dreaded it, and it did not matter that the cause of this morning's argument was so trivial that he had already forgotten it.

Gran'paw's brown hand rested tensely on the blue metal. Frank was on the verge of reaching out to touch it, make it turn so he could grasp it, when Gran'paw spoke. "A week. They been out yonder a week. I went out to the smokehouse for me a slice of bacon and their windows flashed the mornin' sun in my eyes so bright it hurt."

"What're they doin'? They aren't goin' to tear down the house, are they?"

"Widen the road so people can pass the cars about to pull off to gawk at my home."

"Have they been to see you?"

"They stood just out of range and give me till tomorrow. *They*—" He couldn't say it again.

"Can they really do it, Gran'paw?"

"If they can get me a good one between the eyes. No stranger will ever come and stare at this room. Not as long as I've got strength to pull a trigger." He looked out through the curtain as though looking through a small hole in a wall of granite. "They sent that other one first. Promised faithfully he'd get me more than the land's worth. 'Hit's worth your life,' I told him. 'If hit was worth the life of the men that come here—not to die killin' the Indians that owned it, but to die in the winters that come over it, men who come here before they *was* a government, or tourists, either—hit's worth *yours*. Does it mean that much to you?' I asked him. 'Hit's not for *me*,' he said, 'Hit's for all Americans who may come to visit the park and see the way of life you pioneers had here.' 'I still have it,' I says, 'and we didn't none of us come to visit. We come to stay,' and I told him I didn't have nothin' in mind but doin' just that. . . .

"I've a mind to burn it to the ground. Not out of spite. But to keep it from gittin' marked and cut up and stromped over by people from all over the world that's got nothin' to keep 'em at home. Well, I don't mind if they point to a black place on the earth where my house *was*."

"Would you really—?" He started to ask if Gran'paw would shoot to kill, but realized that the question almost said Frank himself wouldn't.

"I don't expect you to stay, son." Frank was hurt that he didn't. Seeing that, Gran'paw said, "I mean—"

"How long you think we can hold up?" It was turning out so much like the movies he had seen, Frank felt silly. He wanted to laugh. But the place where he felt like laughing hurt.

"Long as I've got breath in me. Is it worth it to you, son?" He was trying not to let Frank see his eyes. Frank was here beside him, loaded shotgun clicking lightly against his loaded rifle when he moved, but Gran'paw knew it was hopeless.

"It means enough, and more."

Facing the window, Gran'paw nodded, as if to some-one standing in the road. He shifted and opened the box very slowly and rolled a cartridge between his fingers. A smell came from the box. Frank ran his fingers over the curtain and coughed. The cold room rang like a cell.

"You better put that glove back on," Gran'paw said, seeing that Frank's hand was red on the curtain that dangled over his knee.

Frank put the glove on, pulled it tight. The dogs looked up, and the shepherd got up and turned around and lay down again.

They were quiet. Frank began to feel better. The tension seeped out of him, and the sunlight sopped it up.

Frank looked out the window and clucked softly, as if to say, 'All that snow on the road, they're likely not to come.' Gran'paw looked and looked in his slow, unmoving, thorough way. He didn't reckon they would either, but he kept on sitting.

"Maybe it wouldn't hurt," said Frank, "if I got up and got us some coffee to boiling."

He left the curtain swinging over the shotgun across the cane-bottom chair.

He didn't stop at coffee. He dragged out everything that might smell good and got the fire going blue blazes and loud. In the front of the house, Gran'paw moved around.

Frank went to the door of the parlor, and the dogs' looking up was all that moved, the curtain still, Frank's chair full of light, softening the shotgun.

Peppering the fried potatoes, Frank turned when he heard paws on the linoleum, and saw Gran'paw getting up, in the front of the house.

After breakfast, Gran'paw pushed back and turned his chair toward the kitchen door because both their faces were red from the fire in the stove, and they had started to sweat. "Run me out of the house?" he said, swatting at the hot air that wafted from the stove.

When the fire had settled, Frank sensed it was time.

"They'll get it all, Gran'paw. Let's light out with the cattle and the sheep and the mule and the dogs—up into the mountains."

"High mountains is a whole way of livin' that I don't know, son. High-up mountains with no valleys. They's a few that won't *live* nowhurs else. Like the McCartles."

"They'd be people we could live with."

"They're almost trash, truth of it."

"I thought you liked 'em."

"To hunt with."

"You'd rather live with them than what's comin' in."

Gran'paw thought a long time. Then he got up, and they started to get ready.

Frank rode the mule bareback up a path toward the daylight dark the congested trees made, Gran'paw choosing to trudge on foot behind. As they climbed among the trees, Frank caught glimpses over his shoulder of the level valley below. Rabbits ran over the snow, and large birds, hawks, he hoped, broke the ceiling of pine needles, and Gran'paw said, "Pretty soon we'll see some bears," but Frank thought he was kidding. Although he had seen pictures of them coming up to the windows of cars in the Smokies near Gatlinburg, somehow Frank thought they were part of the tourist lure, trained to return to their cages at dusk.

Beside the path, the dogs took one sniff that was more than enough of the remains of a deer some wildcat had got, the tooth marks still in its throat, the head only still intact after the teeth of many animals had worked over the rest. Snow melted in its nostrils.

Frank had to go afoot and lead the mule now, up the slick, uneven path. At the end of a four-mile climb, he sat down on a rock, mud smeared on his gloves and his jacket sleeves, and up to his knees from slipping suddenly, almost rolling down the steep sides among rocks and lightning-shattered trees, some dead a hundred years, the chestnuts blighted gray. Standing before a thick pine tree that lay across the path, wondering how he was going to get the mule around or over it, Frank watched a bear rise from behind a fern-garnished rock and look at him.

The dogs stopped dead still. Gran'paw murmured to the mule and the dogs. Frank and Gran'paw watched the bear, trying at the same time to calm the animals, to keep the dogs from barking and starting for it. Frank wanted to shoot it, show Gran'paw he had the start of a hunter in him. It just stood there by the rock, making noises, its nose up in the air like a man about to give his neck a few strokes with a razor, and then he rubbed his back up against the sharp edge of the rock, ignoring them, the noise coming from deeper down in his chest, a growl of relief, followed by a moan of contentment. When Frank stepped forward and raised the shotgun to sight, Gran'-paw said, "That's no time for a creature to die," and pressed down the muzzle with two fingers. The bear ambled away among the trees. The woods were quiet. Then a branch snapped as he passed, unseen, deeper inside.

They came out into a small clearing where the snow hadn't melted at all. Frank looked down on a stretch of clouds, broken by the peaks of mountains. On the other side, they broke through some woods to another, smaller clearing among some big trees. A spring shot out of a wall of moss-covered rocks, and a girl, rising with a bucket of dripping water, turned to look at them. Frank's arms were pulled tight backwards—the mule trying to hobble over some small rocks and sticks—and his face had broken out in a sweat. He imagined how he looked to her wearing the motorcycle rig, and was embarrassed, even though she wore a big floppy mustard-green army overcoat that dragged on the snow around her, and on her feet she wore muddy, white majorette boots, the pompon missing on one, a hard, mud-caked lump dangling from the other. The coat hung open, showing her dress, plain yellow cotton that hung so loosely around her waist he got no idea of her breasts or hips, and her blond hair was such a long tangled mess, he couldn't tell how it would look combed out and flowing. The girl of his wildest dreams close up, and he wasn't about to back away from her.

"Is your paw about?" asked Gran'paw.

"Over yonder," she said, pointing. Frank looked. A range of mountains that reached far as he could see.

Frank didn't speak to her. He wanted the first thing he said to make a strong impression. She didn't seem to have Frank on her mind at all, not about to look at him or start to speak. Pulling up on the pail handle with one hand, she stuck the other straight out for balance, and walked into the trees without looking back.

"Pluma McCartle," Gran'paw whispered to Frank. "When it comes to wild, them hogs on Bald Mountain ain't got nothin' on *her*."

The spring shot out of the rocks high above them and splashed right above their heads. Frank drank until he could hardly walk. With the cold ringing in his head, raw in his throat, he went on up, over one crest after another, restraining himself from asking if each were the last. He felt Knoxville being pushed farther and farther back, and every bent limb he let fly was like a door slamming that city and everything in it out.

On a steep cleared place, slung up against a rugged wall of rock, where a few twisted pines grew out of some gashes, was the McCartle house, and eight or nine other smaller shacks covered the slope, a few among the trees, some against other rocks. People and animal feet and rain had smoothed off the yard in front of the porch that set up high on poles cut off the place. Everything looked built right out of the mountain.

A woman came out and looked over the railing. Her arms crossed, stomach pressed against the rail, she looked down at Frank and Gran'paw.

"Afternoon, ma'am," said Gran'paw, taking off his hat. "I was lookin' for Neb."

She squinted at them a long while before she spoke, picking at the faded blue neckline of her dress. "They be back d'reckly. Who be you all?"

"I'm Matthew Hindle and this here is my gran'son Frank. I've knowed Neb McCartle for years."

"Come a long way have ye?"

"Down in the valley way early this mornin'."

"Well, git in this house and pull up to some grub," she said, and went in like she had something to go on now, but she came back to the door when they reached the steep steps, Gran'paw with his hand on Frank's shoulder, and again when they hit the porch.

Pluma sat by the fire in the yellow dress and the major-ette boots, staring into the flames. She didn't seem shy. It wasn't an act such as Frank had seen Knoxville girls put on, and her mother paid Frank and Gran'paw no mind until the food was on the table.

Frank felt as though Gran'paw, in his silent way, was showing him off, but nobody paid any attention. An old coon dog came in once and sniffed at everything and then went out again, but when Frank heard rain on the tin roof, the dog came slinking back in and collapsed like a hairy sack of bones before the fire, and Pluma took one foot out of a boot and put it on the dog's ribs and rubbed it back and forth while the dog whined contentedly. After a while, she smiled and flashed her head back to keep her hair from tickling her cheek. Frank and Gran'paw were wiping their plates when the old man looked up, and they listened to footsteps on the porch—like a herd of ele-phants.

A giant of a man who hadn't shaved in days came tromping in, carrying a shotgun, scattering crumbs of mud before him all the way across the room to the hearth.

More men pushing through stopped up the door behind him. Looking at Frank and Gran'paw, he stood dripping in front of the fire. About ten men filled the room a few moments, then dropped to the floor against the wall when the benches and the places next to Gran'paw and Frank at the table were filled. Nobody spoke. They groaned a little, softly. Frank was looking at men tireder than *he* was. The first one in reached down without really looking at her and pulled Pluma up off the low stool by the arm and gently pushed her aside and sat down himself. Then he looked directly across the room at Gran'paw.

"Well, I tell you, Mr. Hindle, I'm God proud to see you up here."

"I reckon you heared about down yonder."

He nodded and spat into the fire. "I heared, I reckon." He unlaced his boots very slowly, and, so slowly it got on Frank's nerves, lifted them shoulder high and with a flip of his wrist let them fall to the hearth right by the dog's head. Its eyes just rolled up at him, the corners of its mouth sagged open like a fold in leather. Outside, Gran'-paw's dogs and more of the McCartles' pack were barking at each other. The woman stood in the doorway and told the dogs to shut up the racket. Gran'paw got up and went to her side and called his dogs down, pausing a moment in the door after they were quiet, facing out.

"Reckon my people," said Mr. McCartle, "way back in the old time after the flood, got off the ark soon's the water broke on the mountain tops, and only lately have we got down to where it found its level. Now I look down and it seems all that trash is about to rise. Not you. The stuff that's pushin' you up."

Frank sensed that Gran'paw was nervous and uncer-tain, as if he were remembering other trips he had made

up here, with more authority and respect. It didn't seem
to help that the man who was head of this family had
thrown his boots down in sympathy. Frank looked at
McCartle's foot, white on the hearth beside his steaming
boots, Pluma's majorette boots, and the coon dog. In the
room lit only by the fire, something moved from man to
man. Then somebody sitting beside Frank nudged him,
and he turned, looking at the man for the first time. He
put a jug in Frank's hands, so heavy he almost dropped it.
He had to show Frank how. The man—somebody called
him Lufton—seemed to know Frank was ignorant, but
all that meant was that he would have to learn.

Frank was glad when Gran'paw sat down across from
him at the big heavy table again. McCartle passed the
pop-skull whiskey to him and he drank it right the first
time, even though Frank had never seen him take a drink
in the valley. From then on, Frank was out of it. He felt
like the red hot coals that he watched go out and turn
gray.

Pluma became so warm in the glow of Frank's mind
and the fire and the smell of wet clothing steaming and
bodies and sudden sweat and dirt and women and snuff
and pine logs and dogs and guns and old meat and his
own smell that he felt she was soaking him up into her
own body, her yellow dress, and golden hair, and he was
inside her, looking back at himself, sitting, his whole body
throbbing slowly and big, on the bench at the table, held
up by the men on each side of him.

Thunder woke him once and he rose from the floor,
and through one window saw a white flash light up the
porch eaves that dripped heavily, and, far off in the distance, the cold blue of mountains, range after range. All
around him, bodies lay on the floor, some with huge coats

over them, some with quilts, and he felt a wool blanket under his chin. Turning his head on the dusty floor, he saw the last red ember blink out on the hearth.

The next day, Gran'paw told Frank how things were going to be. Neb McCartle and his eight boys were going to help them clear a place about a mile off and put up a cabin. Gran'paw and Frank could live there as long as they wanted to, and they could all hunt and fish together, and they could grow a little something for themselves.

They set about doing it that very morning. Seven axes went out, Frank carrying one with a double edge. They kidded him, telling him to watch out for the wildcats and not to step on the rattlesnakes and to look for bears behind the rocks. Frank felt they didn't like him, but by kidding him they were *trying* to, for Gran'paw's sake. As if they were soldiers, they treated Gran'paw as if he was a general who had fallen off his horse in front of the regiment.

They stopped under some dead locusts that still dripped from last night's rain and Frank heard a fast, hard stream nearby. They cut all morning, the most beautiful sound Frank ever heard. The chopping, the pause, the crash, the pause, the chopping again. When they sat for a rest, Frank noticed that three of the men were missing, and Gran'paw told him they had gone for the livestock left at the end of the road the day before. Frank felt the clearing expand, tree by tree.

Pluma came up with a bucket of water on her head and some cold ham and biscuits in a red and black plaid school satchel. She wore an air force jacket with lamb's wool lining, her hair the same way, her face even dirtier. Frank decided that she just didn't know any better.

By sundown, the place was clear, and when he walked among the fallen trees to the other side where the others had been cutting, he saw the stream he had listened to all day.

When they went in for supper, Frank saw Gran'paw's livestock, tied to trees all around the house. Mr. McCartle said there wasn't any grazing land, except what they would have after the clearing was done, and that was very little. Gran'paw said he and Frank would continue to cut trees until winter set in hard, and cut more in the spring, and "pass the red-eye gravy, please." It would never be good grazing, he told Frank, but it would keep them alive. Neb said let's eat the cattle and sheep this winter, then Gran'paw could devote all his time to hunting. When Gran'paw claimed he was a farmer, they all laughed, until each one caught the look in his eyes.

The rest of the evening, Gran'paw avoided Frank's eyes, and Frank stayed away from him.

The wagon was out in the yard. One of the sons said they took it apart and hauled it up on their backs and now couldn't put it back together again. "Where's a wagon going to go to up on this mountain, anyway?" asked Lufton, and they all laughed.

That night, Frank expected them to sit around the fire and sing old timey songs and tell stories about the old days, but all they did was sit and talk trifles. Pluma hardly looked Frank's way.

As they were walking back to the cabin, Frank said, "Tell me 'bout Daddy when he lived with *you*."

"Now I've told you before, Son, that's too much fer me to dig up again. Let it stay buried. That was before your time."

"*I* ain't *got* no time. They's things I got to get settled in my mind. The way I know my father now, they's too much hard feelin'."

"I knowed him that way, too."

"But *before* is what I mean."

"Before what?"

"He met my mother."

"You don't need to hear all that."

"Please. And then we'll go to bed."

"Tonight, then, but don't ever mention him to me again."

"I promise."

"It hurts too much to remember that boy the way he was before *she* come along. I guess when all the other children left, I looked to him fer too much. And then when his momma died . . . ." Suddenly, he looked up. "Frank, the thing was, he was the only one. He was a good and gentle boy. But he was too weak."

Gran'paw didn't speak for a long time, and Frank settled into silence, giving it up.

"1923. They was a big race riot in Knoxville that year. He told me all about it. We got so we had to haul produce to Market Square to have enough money to do. Never went myse'f. Him and Jake Norton loaded up Jake's T-model truck and ever' mornin' in the summer of '23, they'd drag that contraption to Knoxville and sell tamaters n' corn n' walnuts and things. Even painted it orange so folks could see 'em sittin' there. Well, the way he told it was that him and Jake ducked inside this Gold Sun Café to get out of the way of the shootin'—they had sol'jers on the roofs with machine guns when this riot was goin' on. That's where he met Geneva Clayborne, in that café. First thing I knowed he couldn't draw breath without first callin' her name. Made me sick to hear it. Then he brung her home in that orange truck, 'cause he'd just got done marryin' her in Mar'vul. He wasn't the same no more after *that*. That girl just set around the house, hardly liftin' her finger to do any work, and moped about Knoxville and her people that all works in them mills down yonder. She weren't a damn bit like his momma. I couldn't never understand it. Then one day she run off—got a ride with Jake on his veg'table truck. I ain't never seen her since and I don't keer to, neither. He lit out lookin' fer her after 'bout a week a-moanin' around. Bought Jake's truck and lit out. I told 'im not to ever come back if he took up with her agin. He knowed I meant it. I reckon thet's what he done, 'cause I ain't seen 'im since."

Gran'paw gazed into the fire, as though trying to find something he had misplaced. Poking it with a small, curved branch, he stopped and looked up at the ceiling. "No, come to think, that ain't right. They *did* come back. I was sittin' on the porch whittlin' me a pin for the wagon when I seen that orange truck come up the road, and I thought, I ort to *know* that truck. They stopped out front and I just looked at them. He stayed behind the wheel and leaned across in front of her and yelled, with the biggest grin on his face, that he had him a farm outside Knoxville and wanted me to see it. I just looked at him, and then after about five minutes, he went on up the road and turned around and drove back by. By that time, I was in the house. I don't know what they come to see *me* for."

But from the time he could listen, Frank had known, and then when he reached a time when he thought he could walk it, he had set out in the snow for Cades Cove, trembling with fear, wanting to see the man who had been the invisible mover of his father's, of his momma's, of his own life. But that orange truck had caught up with him at the city limits on the opposite end of Knoxville. Then six months ago, kicked out of school for truancy, fleeing his father's wrath, his mother's tears, sick of his motorcycle club, The Hellhounds, dreading the draft, he fled Knoxville, seeking a haven in Cades Cove. All his life he had listened to his father talk about Gran'paw Hindle and Cades Cove, and now he was finally going.

Gran'paw's unwillingness to forgive his father scared Frank.

For more than a week, Frank and Gran'paw worked on the cabin by the stream, and the McCartles did less and less and left more of it up to Frank and Gran'paw. But when the cabin was finished, they all came loping in and sat on the floor against the wall and passed the jug to celebrate. As the whiskey got low, they turned to talk to keep them high, and Lufton was moved to sing. Frank asked him to sing it again so he could follow the words.

Run, Jack, run, with Pluma through the night;
Into the mountains and out of sight.
Don't let the chiggers, snakes, and sheriff bother you,
Run with your sweetheart into the mountains blue.

"Oh, hell's fire," said Mr. McCartle, "you ain't no song-maker, boy. Sing him the one that's spread over the whole stretch of the Smokies." He winked at Frank. "Lufton keeps trying to make up a better one. Thinks just because it's his sister, he knows more what a song it ort to be."

The singer stared at his father in mock disbelief, his mouth gaping, his eyes bugged. Then he looked ordinary, and said, "Well, then *you* sing it. I ain't *about* to."

"When I learn to sing sweet enough the vultures flock

to listen, you come around and I'll croon that'n off for you."

"This is a song about Pluma?" asked Frank. "About her and some boy named Jack?"

"You mean you ain't heard?" Henry asked. "Down yonder in the big o' city a Knoxville?"

They kidded Frank awhile, then, in a soft voice that seemed to go with the cooing of a dove outside and the rhythm of the stream, Lufton told him.

"Pluma ain't been sprung from jail more'n a month. We all had to hoof it down to Mar'vul and put up a thousand-dollar bond, that what folks we know good, and our relatives, same thing, throwed together for us to take down the mountain. She's loved the fool out of that Jack Standridge since she was eleven. He never knowed nothin' but draggin' old jalopies up the mountain and tryin' to get them back down after he was done foolin' with them. He's one for findin' him a parked car with a key in it and takin' a all night ride. Well, he met this woman twenty years older'n him that had a good Buick her husband left her when he got on that old Gospel ship and sailed away—"

"Tell it without that smartness, Lufton," said McCartle.

"Yes, sir. So she held that Buick over him and made him keep regular hours and had him a nervous wreck before he could put 1000 mile of his own on that speedometer. Well, one dry time, he made it to the end of the road *you* all left, and he come up to see Pluma to show off his Buick. Pluma made him wait till she could show off a thing or two herself." McCartle slapped Lufton. Lufton took a swig and went on. "Enough till he didn't know whether it was the car made him take those curves like a kid tryin' to keep from peein' in his pants or *her,* pushed up against him so hard the door handle punctured his ribs, seemed like. You don't want to ever see that young'un loop her leg over your knee. *He* did, and put on about 300 mile that Sunday, showin' her—" McCartle finally reached him to slap him again, and Lufton took a swig, and went on. "Then—" He stopped and looked at his daddy. "Say, paw, don't you like this blamed story or not?"

"Sure, I love to hear you tell it, so I can lam you up 'gin the head ever' time you throw off on your sister."

"Throw *off?* More like *up.* Okay! Claim you hit me, then *don't.* Well, howsom'ever, Jack's near-gray-headit wife, this Ora Lee Morgan, caught wind of that ride. Don't you know she pistol-whupped that poor boy till he must a wondered which tore him up more, ridin' in that brand new Buick, sittin' hip-connected to Pluma, or gettin' marked up by his till-death-do-us-partner. Well, 'bout a hour later, he picked hisself up and went out to the garage to make one of them getaways like in the picture show and when he opened the garage door, reckon what he saw? A woman with her head konked on the wheel. Reckon who it was? Ora Lee Morgan, the very one. Reckon what he done?"

"Goddamn it, Lufton!" McCartle started to hit him again.

"Scooted her over and backed on out. Knocked one door clean off the hinges and carried it to the city limits on his hood. Come to the end of the road at the foot of our mountain, and reckon what this time? Mud, butt deep. So he pulls her out and sets her up agin a tree and tries it with a lighter car. Mud sucked it in deeper. Come up the path and got Pluma out of the bed. We was asleep.

It was way early. Not a livin' eye open. Less you count mine."

"And didn't try to stop her," said McCartle.

"Why should I? I'm the worst one in the world for wantin' to see how a thing's gonna turn out. If I could read, I'd give up my huntin'. So back down they went. But by that time the Sheriff was there. Somebody seen that car go down the streets of Mar'vul at four A.M. with a garage door floppin' on the hood. Jack and Pluma lit *out* before they seen—or you might say *up*. Then down. Then up. Up and down these mountains for a month, bless your soul. See, Jack figured the Sheriff would think he had stuck his wife in the car and left the motor running and give her a whiff of that what-you-call-it folks get when they shut themselfs up in garages and let the motor run. And reckon what? That feller took up stealin', too. Or really worked at it, bein' a thief the least bit before."

"Just to eat, Lufton," said McCartle. "Don't you eat, too?"

"Yeah, but not other folks' rations. Slipped into stores. Slipped into houses even. And folks' crops. Nothin' like that to turn a body agin you. Unless the law gets folks even madder. Which was what they done. Which was what they done." Lufton paused.

"What did they do?" Frank asked.

"They brung in them hellercopters and state troopers and bloodhounds and radios, and covered these mountains. That wasn't so bad. Folks loved to watch all that commotion. But then they started runnin' into a couple a stills folks has been runnin' for generations. And they decided they was madder at the law than they was at Jack and Pluma. Well, to keep from makin' a short story long, they found them one day in the heat of August, sleepin' under a shade tree. First, they had to beat a nest of copperheads to death and that was what woke Jack and Pluma up. They say them two put up a better fight than the copperheads done. Well, the trial come up pretty quick, and it turned out the jury thought Ora Lee died of an accident—of breathing them fumes. They charged Jack and Pluma with the stuff they pilfered and the cars they swiped, while they was runnin'. Jack made such a pretty speech about how he sure wished he could go in the army and serve his country that the Judge said he'd turn him loose if Jack would sign up. Let Pluma off, too, if her paw would keep her out of young married men's cars."

"You want me to crock you one with this jug?"

"Not till I ask you. So Jack signed on the dotted and they told him it'd *be* a few days before he had to go, so he come up here to see Pluma, and they took out again and started it all over again. But this time the army drug him off. And now Pluma just stands around, waitin' for him to come up that mountain, draggin' his medals. That song I won't sing was wrote before they was ever caught the first time. I'm still writin' on mine. Gonna be on the Gran' Ol' Opry before I'm done."

"Thet boy ain't never satisfied."

"Once you're borned, ain't you done lost the last chance't to be?"

"Sing your song again," Frank said.

"Sing it, hell. I done *told* it now. Pass me that jug."

McCartle, a grin breaking across his face, passed his son the empty jug.

Then everyone got quiet and a sudden dead-serious tone set in.

Gran'paw asked if there was anything in the world he could do to repay them for their help, and McCartle kept saying nothing, forget it, until time to leave, and then he said, yes, he'd take one of the cows. Gran'paw tried to talk him into something else, but McCartle just went out among the stumps and took one of the cows with him into the trees, Lufton and the other boys ambling behind.

Frank lay awake that night in the dark, thinking Gran'-paw was asleep.

"My blackest fears," said Gran'paw suddenly, "is that they'll come down and root in the graveyard."

"Who?"

"Them wild hogs comin' down off the Bald."

"You keep talkin' 'bout 'em, but I can't feature where they're at."

"Why, up on Rich Mountain, on the Balds, son, they's meadows five thousand feet up, where all the folks in the valley used to take the cattle. Hardly a sign left of the herders' cabins now. But thirty years after the last of the wanderin' herders was gone, the stink of ramps in the cabins would lift you off your feet at the threshold. *That's* a onion that'll strong ye. Me and your daddy used to go up there to hunt wild hogs that breed amongst the little trees that overrun the meadows. These wild hogs is a cross between the boars our daddies brought over from Scotland and the pigs we raised in the valley. Well, they're all roamin' the Balds this very night, rootin' up the young trees, and I'm afeared they'll go down like they done one bad winter and root in the graveyard where your gran'-maw's buried."

The next morning, Frank woke Gran'paw. "Let's go up and kill 'em off."

"Kill what off?"

"Let's go up and kill off those hogs."

"You ever shoot a shotgun with wild hogs chargin' you?"

"No, sir, not yet."

Gran'paw thought a long time. Then he flung back the covers and got up, and they started to get ready.

When they broke out of the woods onto the Bald, the sky was the purple dark of a bruise, and one vast curve reached from their feet to the horizon. The trees were runty and had turned to ice. Frank saw acres of blue-silver limbs, and twigs stirred in the wind, a sound like faint chimes that all together made a loud commotion of crystal. The mule seemed shocked at the sight, and the dogs whimpered. They had taken one step off the edge of the world, and this was what it was like—a maze of identical ice trees.

The barrels of Frank's and Gran'paw's shotguns clicked together and startled them.

"Keep a distance," murmured Gran'paw, as though it were some magic formula to ward off evil. He had returned to a place he had once known, but he breathed and moved like an absolute stranger.

The sky turned black and the moon came up. Each footstep in the snow, as they moved among the twigs of ice that scratched against their shoulders, made a distinct crunch.

Frank and Gran'paw stopped. Frank heard them clearly when the dogs took one step further, and stopped, and looked, as if they had possibly taken one step too many.

A shape unlike the trees showed through the branches ahead. One of the shacks. It leaned crookedly where it had sunk in the spongy ground in the thirty or forty springs since its door was last shut. A veneer of ice.

As Gran'paw opened the door, a sound like a cracking of glass wound around the frame.

Frank unpacked the dry wood they had brought on the mule.

He stepped over the sill and tripped and sprawled over the hard dirt floor of the cabin. The floor had sunk and it tilted.

Gran'paw let the mule come in with the dogs, and the fire stirred up some heat that made the ice weep at the small windowpane.

They didn't speak. Gran'paw seemed to be listening, too. Frank imagined enormous white hogs with bluish icicles for tusks stampeding the cabin, mangling it under their hooves.

Frank and Gran'paw didn't go out looking for the hogs. They slept near the dogs and the mule, and kept the fire glowing throughout the night. The stir of wind in the ice trees made them sleep in fits and starts. The light of the false dawn on the window, Frank woke to the snuffling, snorting sound of snouts. Gran'paw was up, the shotgun in his hands. Hooves clattered against the boards and made the icicles clash and fall. The wood walls muffled a surly squeal when an icicle struck one of them.

The mule wanted out.

The dogs were terrified and vicious.

Gran'paw fired his shotgun through the four walls as quickly as he could and when the reverberations quieted, they listened to the hooves and the falling splinters of ice as the hogs fled. The walls were soft as peat and he had blown large holes in them.

Frank and Gran'paw sat a few hours by the fire, smelling the ghostly, rank odor of ramps and watching powdery snow blow in through the holes.

When they began the long descent the next afternoon, they left the Bald studded with the stiffening bodies of wild hogs as the ice on the trees cracked and dripped off the branches and twigs and slid in shards down the black trees upon the carcasses and the blood.

"They'll be there a long time," said Gran'paw. "Buzzards don't expect much up this high. Tend to favor the valley. Least I'll know where they are when I pass the graveyard below."

"Then we killed them all?"

"No, but we got the ones we saw."

With the smell of blood and animal death and gunpowder and ice and ramps on his clothes and his boots and his hands, Frank walked down the mountain, off the Bald, Gran'paw riding the mule behind, for he was very tired and seemed much older.

Frank knew that Gran'paw was ashamed now to have him around. He told Gran'paw that he would make McCartle give the cow back if he thought he would need it, but Gran'paw acted as though Frank didn't know any better than to talk that way.

Lying next to Gran'paw in the one, narrow bed, Frank began to remember Knoxville and his father and his mother, and the Hellhounds, and the draft notice. But he wanted to stay up here and be part of Gran'paw and this life, so he tried to shut everything about Knoxville out of his mind.

One morning, he went up on the McCartle front porch and found the Sunday Knoxville *News-Sentinel*, spread out on the bench with the bright, cold sunlight on it. Although it was very cold that November morning, he sat down and turned through the paper. On the front page, the war in Vietnam was going very badly for the United States. He read a little piece about a boy from Rule High who had volunteered, and it made him sneer. Feeling somebody standing in the doorway, he turned and Pluma was looking at him. Her hair was combed neatly, her face was smooth and clean. She wore red ballerina shoes, rocking on the sill.

"What does it say?"

"You mean the paper?"

She nodded and came out on the porch, and leaned against the railing, facing Frank.

"About the war and all kinds of things."

"Which one?"

"In Vietnam."

She frowned and thought a while and then her face brightened. "Overseas?"

"Yeah."

"Do *you* have to go?"

"Not yet."

"I don't see why *he* has to, if *you* don't."

"Who is *he*?"

"Jack."

Frank pretended that Steve Canyon caught his eye. She pushed off from the rail and went inside, and Frank sat on the bench against the front of the house, depressed. He folded the paper neatly, and was about to lay it aside and get up and go, when she came out again with a white bag balanced on the palm of her hand. Chewing, she offered Frank some of what was in the bag. He reached in and felt jellybeans.

"No thanks."

"*Better*, while the grabbin's good. It'll be snow in *July* 'fore the next batch. They sendin' him to V-nam or ever what you call it, and my blamed brothers won't trifle with such when they go down."

"He home now?"

"Come last night and brung us that newspaper and a poke of jellybeans and me a pillow." She went in again and brought out the pillow. "Can you read that?"

Frank had never met an illiterate before. Even Gran'-paw wasn't. "To my Sweetheart from Fort Jackson, South Carolina."

"It's of Hawaii." She ran her fingers over the palm trees, the huts, and the lagoon, then flicked at the orange fringe.

"You like it?"

"It's all right." She set the bag on the rail and hugged the pillow to her belly. "He said he slept with his head on it comin' up on the bus." She sniffed it and when she put it back over her belly, Frank saw the glaze of hair oil. She wore a skinny belt now and her shape showed in the soft cotton dress. Frank was so jealous he could scarcely see her, and when she slid along the rail, her head uncovered the sun and it glared into Frank's eyes.

"You look good with your hair that way." But that didn't do anything to her.

She threw and Frank caught a licorice jellybean. It made him sick because he hadn't eaten anything yet.

"I wished they'd make 'em *all* black," she said, stirring around the bottom of the bag.

"I bet you'd love to go to Market Square in Knoxville."

"I been."

"You like it?"

"I like it up *here*."

"You must not of stayed in Market Square *long*."

"They got mad at me because I said I was goin' to strike out afoot if they didn't bring me back."

"What didn't you like about it?"

"Nothin'. I like it up here and no place else."

"Does your boyfriend?"

"He was borned and raised over the mountain."

"Wait till he's been to Japan. They say when a boy from the hills of Tennessee gets done seein' Tokyo, he's rur'n't for anything but roamin'. Come up the path with one a them slant-eyed girls." Frank expected her to flare up at him, but she looked at him as if what he said made no sense.

"He likes it same as me. When he gets back, him and me's goin' to live higher up. We like it up where it's good and cold." When she jerked the bag holding the jellybeans back toward a mountain that rose above the others in the blue mist to the clouds, a black one popped out of the bag.

Frank knew she meant it, and that Jack would come back, and they would go up there and build a cabin and hunt. And he knew that *he* never would. He liked it up here, too, but he knew, sitting there with the Knoxville *News-Sentinel* spread over his knees, that he wouldn't like it any higher up as long as he gave a damn that his life in Knoxville was falling apart.

He went back to the cabin and helped Gran'paw start putting together another bed, but somehow they lost interest and left the job to catch some trout for supper.

When Frank strolled back up to the McCartle place that evening, the old man was chopping wood, and the boys were sitting around watching him, but Pluma and her boyfriend were nowhere in sight.

Dipping some drinking water out of the stream that night, Frank saw a flashlight flicker way up on the mountain. Pluma and Jack were up there, coming down from the top.

When Frank woke up the next morning, Gran'paw was not in the cabin. Walking around outside, Frank called the dogs and looked into the trees but did not see the old man. He walked through the woods to the stream and looked up and down, whistling and calling the dogs. Staring into the rippling reflections in the clear water just before he doused his face to wake himself up, Frank felt certain that Gran'paw had gone off and left him, determined never to return. As the icy water struck his face, he felt that Gran'paw was right to leave this mountain. The life they had been setting up here seemed to move away from the dream Frank had always had of Cades Cove and the mountains. For a moment, he resented Gran'paw's action, as if he had betrayed the dream. But then he realized that by feeling so quickly and keenly that Gran'paw had gone for good, Frank himself was betraying lack of faith in the dream. He went up to the McCartle house, imagining Gran'paw sitting on the porch with Neb.

All the McCartles, except Pluma, sat on the porch in the shade or were occupied about the yard in the sun.

"Mr. McCartle, you see my gran'paw?"

"Not since yesterday."

"I can't find him *no*where."

"Oh, he'll come around."

Frank stayed close to the cabin all day, but Gran'paw didn't show up. At about four o'clock, he heard somebody on the path, coming through the trees toward the cabin. Frank called the dogs, forcing a hopeful, happy tone.

Mr. McCartle broke through the pines into the clearing, two hounds at his heels.

"I got 'em trained not to come to nobody's call but mine. Mr. Hindle showed up yet?"

"No, sir. I been waitin'."

"I'uz afeared he wouldn't. I got to studyin' over him, and you know, when old folks get old, they commence to act up."

"Don't reckon he went back home, do you?"

"*Some* would. But I don't feature *him*. He's diff'runt from the rest I've seed. Too proud to slink back down to the valley—too proud to be beholden to *my* outfit."

In front of his house, McCartle organized a search. "I seed it a-comin'," he said, and his boys responded silently, as if they had heard his predictions often.

"Who do *I* go with, sir?" asked Frank.

"By yourse'f—down the trail to where you come from, boy."

"I ought to *be* here when he comes back. I'm the only one he's got."

"That's worse than none. I ain't running *no*body off, but...."

"Nobody loves advice, Paw," said Lufton.

"I know *two* that don't," said McCartle, setting off.

They all went separate ways, and Frank returned to the cabin. Lying on the bunk, aware of the unfinished one across the room, he listened to McCartle's dogs yelping, distracted from the search by wild animals. Watching the room grow dark, he listened to a mild breeze play through the pines. He couldn't keep his mind fixed on Gran'paw. Knoxville and his father and mother and the draft intruded insistently.

A hand shook his shoulder. Moonlight pouring through the only window clearly revealed Lufton. "Wake the hell up, boy."

"Did they find him?"

"*I* found him. Them others ain't no good at story-tellin', singin', or lost gran'paw-findin'."

"Where *is* he then?"

"Right where I found him. I ain't fool enough to try rootin' him out of there."

"Out of where?"

"That deserted herder's cabin up on the Bald. I never seen so many dead hogs in all my borned days. He must a used that shotgun he turned on *me*. Screamed at me, 'This here's *my* mountain now!' For *my* part, he can keep it till the judgment. Got lost up yonder myse'f one time when I'uz a kid—no, I reckon I'uz bout twenty-one, but scareder'n a kid. They used to tell of the wild hogs in this pretty place, and you know *me*, I had to see it. Smelled 'em, but never saw hair *one*. Then tonight all of 'em dead in the moonlight, and Mr. Hindle lordin' it over all creation, seemed like. Them *dogs* even sounded diff'runt. That place'll turn you around. I ain't never been the same myse'f. You ort to see some a my nightmares."

"Did he ask about *me*?"

"Did he ask about *you*? Boy, the onliest thing Mr. Hindle asked *me* was did I want to lay down with them hogs."

"You reckon he'll come back in a few days?"

"A body don't *come* back from where *he's* at. He's out of *this* world and in sight of another."

"You tryin' to say you think he's gone crazy?"

"No, but he's set his mind on the Bald, so he mize *well* be."

"I better go up there and see him in the mornin'. Maybe in the daylight—"

"Daylight or dark, he'll hate to see *you*. Why you reckon he went up yonder in the *first* place? I ain't one to give somebody from Knoxville advice . . . ."

"Thanks, Lufton. I 'preciate you comin' to tell me."

"Oh, I love to *tell* it—it's climbin' them mountains that kills *me*."

Lufton left the cabin, singing:

Run, Jack, run with Pluma through the night;
Into the mountains and out of sight. . . .

As he listened to Lufton and the song fade into the trees, Frank realized that Lufton wanted him to take the song down the mountain and into Knoxville with him.

Frank couldn't go back to sleep. As he lay back on the bunk he and Gran'paw had made, in the cabin they had built, with the help of the McCartles, he remembered something he once read about Eskimos when they get too old to take care of themselves, when they become dependent upon their folks. One day the family wakes up and the old one is gone. The image came to Frank of an ancient Eskimo sitting alone on an ice floe in the arctic night, armed against the ice and snow and stalking beasts and long darkness with a piece of whale blubber. The image persisted as daylight filled the cabin.

Halfway down, Frank heard Pluma and Jack, riding the roads in the valley below, the muffler on his car shot.

Frank's motorcycle was still in the barn. The house was untouched, except that work on the road had caked the windows and sealed up the door over the sill with dust. Frank raised some of it himself when he left Cades

Cove, Knoxville bound, with not the least notion of what he was going to do tomorrow. That put him right back among the people, in the place, in the fix he had run away from a few weeks before.

No Trace

*G*ASPING for air, his legs weak from the climb up the stairs, Ernest stopped outside the room, surprised to find the door wide open, almost sorry he had made it before the police. An upsurge of nausea, a wave of suffocation forced him to suck violently for breath as he stepped into Gordon's room—his *own* two decades before.

Tinted psychedelic emerald, the room looked like a hippie pad posing for a photograph in *Life,* but the monotonous electronic frenzy he heard was the seventeen-year locusts, chewing spring leaves outside. He wondered whether the sedative had so dazed him that he had stumbled into the wrong room. No, now, as every time in his own college years when he had entered this room, what struck him first was the light falling through the leaded, green-stained windowglass. As the light steeped him in the ambience of the early forties, it simultaneously illuminated the artifacts of the present. Though groggy from the sedative, he experienced, intermittently, moments of startling clarity when he saw each object separately.

Empty beer can pyramids.

James Dean, stark poster photograph.

Records leaning in orange crate.

Life-sized redheaded girl, banjo blocking her vagina, lurid color.

Rolltop desk, swivel chair, typewriter.

Poster photograph of a teen-age hero he didn't recognize.

Large CORN FLAKES carton.

Ernest recognized nothing, except the encyclopedias, as Gordon's. Debris left behind when Gordon's roommate ran away. Even so, knowing Gordon, Ernest had expected the cleanest room in DeLozier Hall, vacant except for suitcases sitting in a neat row, awaiting the end-of-ceremonies dash to the car. He shut the door quietly, listening to an automatic lock catch, as if concealing not just the few possible incriminating objects he had come to discover but the entire spectacle of a room startlingly overpopulated with objects, exhibits, that might bear witness, like archeological unearthings, to the life lived there.

He glanced into the closet. Gordon's suitcases did not have the look of imminent departure. Clothes hung, hangers crammed tightly together, on the rack above. The odor emanating from the closet convulsed him slightly, making him shut his eyes, see Gordon raise his arm, the sleeve of his gown slip down, revealing his white arm, the grenade in his hand. Shaking his head to shatter the image, Ernest opened his eyes.

Turning abruptly from the closet, he moved aimlessly about the room, distracted by objects that moved toward him. He had to hurry before someone discovered the cot downstairs empty, before police came to lock up Gordon's room. The green light drew him to the window where the babel of locusts was louder. Through the antique glass, he saw, as if under water, the broken folding chairs below, parodying postures into which the explosion had thrown the audience. The last of the curiosity seekers, turning away, trampling locusts, left three policemen alone among knocked over chairs.

I AM ANONYMOUS/ HELP ME. Nailed, buttons encrusted the windowframe. SUPPORT MENTAL HEALTH OR I'LL KILL YOU. SNOOPY FOR PRESIDENT. As he turned away, chalked, smudged lettering among the buttons drew him back: DOCTOR SPOCK IS AN ABORTIONIST. After his roommate ran away, why hadn't Gordon erased that? Jerking his head away from the buttons again, Ernest saw a ballpoint pen sticking up in the desk top. On a piece of paper, the title "The Theme of Self-hatred in the Works of—" the rest obscured by a blue circular, a message scrawled in lipstick across it: GORDY BABY, LET ME HOLD SOME BREAD FOR THIS CAUSE. MY OLD LADY IS SENDING ME A CHECK NEXT WEEK. *THE* CARTER. The circular pleaded for money for the Civil Liberties Union. Ernest shoved it aside, but "The Theme of Self-hatred in the Works of—" broke off anyway. Gordon's blue scrapbook, green in the light, startled him. Turning away, Ernest noticed REVOLUTION IN A REVOLUTION? A TOLKIEN READER, BOY SCOUT HANDBOOK in a bookcase.

As he stepped toward the closet, something crunching harshly underfoot made him jump back. Among peanut shells, brown streaks in the green light. Gordon tracking smashed guts of locusts. Fresh streaks, green juices of leaves acid-turned to slime. He lifted one foot, trying to look at the sole of his shoe, lost balance, staggered backward, let himself drop on the edge of a cot. If investigators compared the stains—. Using his handkerchief, he wiped the soles. Dying and dead locusts, *The*

Alumni Bulletin had reported, had littered the campus paths for weeks. Everywhere, the racket of their devouring machinery, the reek of their putrefaction when they fell, gorged. Sniffing his lapels, he inhaled the stench of locusts and sweat, saw flecks of—. He shut his eyes, raked breath into his lungs, lay back on the cot.

Even as he tried to resist the resurgent power of the sedative, Ernest felt his exhausted mind and body sink into sleep. When sirens woke him, he thought for a moment he still lay on the bare mattress in the room downstairs, listening to the siren of that last ambulance. The injured, being carried away on stretchers, passed by him again. The Dean of Men had hustled Ernest into a vacated room, and sent to his house nearby for a sedative. Sinking into sleep, seeing the grenade go off again and again until the explosions became tiny, receding, mute puffs of smoke, Ernest had suddenly imagined Lydia's face when he would have to telephone her about Gordon, and the urgency of being prepared for the police had made him sit up in the bed. The hall was empty, everyone seemed to be outside, and he had sneaked up the narrow back stairway to Gordon's room.

Wondering which cot was Gordon's, which his roommate's, and why *both* had recently been slept in, Ernest sat up and looked along the wooden frame for the cigarette burn he had deliberately made the day before his own commencement when he and his roommate were packing for home. As he leaned across the cot, looking for the burn, his hand grazed a stiff yellow spot on the sheet. The top sheet stuck to the bottom sheet. An intuition of his son's climactic moment in an erotic dream the night before—the effort to keep from crying choked him. "I advocate—." Leaping away from the cot, he stopped, reeling, looked up at a road sign that hung over the door: DRIVE SLOWLY, WE LOVE OUR KIDS. Somewhere an unprotected street. What's-his-name's fault. *His* junk cluttered the room.

Wondering what the suitcases would reveal, Ernest stepped into the closet. Expecting them to be packed, he jerked up on them and jolted himself, they were so light. He opened them anyway. Crumbs of dirt, curls of lint. Gordon's clothes, that Lydia had helped him select, or sent him as birthday or Easter presents, hung in the closet, pressed. Fetid clothes Gordon's roommate—Carter, yes, Carter—had left behind dangled from hooks, looking more like costumes. A theatrical black leather jacket, faded denim pants, a wide black belt, ruby studs, a jade velvet cape, and, on the floor, boots and sandals. In a dark corner leaned the hooded golf clubs Ernest had handed down to Gordon, suspecting he would never lift them from the bag. "You don't like to hunt," he had blurted out one evening. "You don't like to fish. You don't get excited about football. Isn't there *some*thing we could do together?" "We could just sit and talk." They had ended up watching the Ed Sullivan Show.

Ernest's hand, paddling fish-like among the clothes in the dim closet, snagged on a pin that fastened a price tag to one of the suits he had bought Gordon for Christmas. Though he knew from Lydia that no girl came regularly on weekends from Melbourne's sister college to visit Gordon, surely he had had some occasion to wear the suit. Stacked on the shelf above: shirts, the cellophane packaging unbroken. His fingers inside one of the cowboy boots, Ernest stroked leather that was still flesh soft. Imagining Lydia's hysteria at the sight of Gordon, he saw a mortician handling Gordon's body, sorting, arranging pieces, saw not Gordon's, but the body of one of his clients on view, remembering how awed he had been by the miracle of skill that had put the man back together only three days after the factory explosion. Ernest stroked a damp polo shirt, unevenly stained pale green in the wash, sniffed it, realizing that Carter's body could not have left an odor that lasting. Now he understood what had disturbed him about Gordon's clothes, showing, informal and ragged, under the skirt of the black gown, at the sleeves, at the neck, as he sat on the platform, waiting to deliver the valedictory address.

Gripping the iron pipe that held hangers shoved tightly together, his body swinging forward as his knees sagged, Ernest let the grenade explode again. Gentle, almost delicate, Gordon suddenly raises his voice above the nerve-wearying shrill of the seventeen-year locusts that encrust the barks of the trees, a voice that had been too soft to be heard except by the men on the platform whose faces expressed shock—at *what* Ernest still did not know—and as that voice screams, a high-pitched nasal screech like brass, "I advocate a total revolution!" Gordon's left arm raises a grenade, holds it out before him, eclipsing his still-open mouth, and in his right hand, held down stiff at his side, the pin glitters on his finger. Frightened, raring back, as Ernest himself does, in their seats, many people try to laugh the grenade off as a bold but imprudent rhetorical gesture.

Tasting again Gordon's blood on his mouth, Ernest thrust his face between smothering wool coats, retched again, vomited at last.

As he tried to suck air into his lungs, gluey bands of vomit strangled him, lack of oxygen smothered him. Staggering backward out of the closet, he stood in the middle of the room, swaying. Avoiding Gordon's, he lowered himself carefully onto the edge of Carter's cot by the closet. He craved air but the stained-glass window, the only window in this corner room, wouldn't open, a disadvantage that came with the privilege of having the room with the magnificent light. The first time he had seen the room since his own graduation—he and Lydia had brought Gordon down to begin his freshman year—he had had to heave breath up from dry lungs to tell Gordon about the window. Early in the nineteenth century when DeLozier Hall was the entire school—and already one of the finest boys' colleges in the midwest—this corner room and the two adjacent comprised the chapel. From the fire that destroyed DeLozier Hall in 1938, three years before Ernest himself arrived as a freshman, only this window was saved. Except for the other chapel windows, DeLozier had been restored, brick by brick, exactly as it was originally. "First chance you get, go look in the cemetery at the grave of the only victim of the fire—nobody knows who it was, so the remains were never claimed. Probably somebody just passing through." He had deliberately saved that to leave Gordon with something interesting to think about. From the edge of the cot, he saw the bright eruption of vomit on Gordon's clothes.

The chapel steeple chimed four o'clock. The racket of the locusts' mandibles penetrated the room as if carried in through the green light. Photosynthesis. Chlorophyll. The D+ in biology that wrecked his average.

Rising, he took out his handkerchief and went into the closet. When the handkerchief was sopping wet, he dropped it into a large beer carton, tasting again the foaming beer at his lips, tingling beads on his tongue in the hot tent on the lawn as the ceremonies were beginning. He had reached the green just as the procession was forming. "You've been accepted by Harvard Grad School." Gordon had looked at him without a glimmer of recognition—Ernest had assumed that the shrilling of the locusts had drowned out his voice—then led his classmates toward the platform.

Ernest was standing on a dirty tee shirt. He finished the job with that, leaving a corner to wipe his hands on, then he dropped it, also, into the carton.

He sat on the edge of the cot again, afraid to lie back on the mattress, sink into the gulley Carter had made over the four years and fall asleep. He only leaned back, propped on one arm. Having collected himself, he would make a thorough search, to prepare himself for whatever the police would find, tag, then show him for final identification. An exhibit of shocks. The police might even hold him responsible somehow—delinquently ignorant of his son's habits, associates. They might even find something that would bring in the F.B.I.—membership in some radical organization. What was *not* possible in a year like this? He had to arm himself against interrogation. "What sort of boy was your son?" "Typical, average, normal boy in every way. Ask my wife." But how many times had he read that in newspaper accounts of monstrous crimes? What did it mean anymore to be normal?

Glancing around the room, on the verge of an unsettling realization, Ernest saw a picture of Lydia leaning on Carter's rolltop desk. Even in shadow, the enlarged snapshot he had taken himself was radiant. A lucid April sunburst in the budding trees behind her, bleached her green dress white, made her blond hair look almost platinum. Clowning, she had kicked out one foot, upraising and spreading her arms, and when her mouth finished yelling "Spring!" he had snapped her dimpled smile. On the campus of Melbourne's sister college Briarheath, locusts riddled those same trees, twenty years taller, forty miles from where he sat, while Lydia languished in bed alone— a mysterious disease, a lingering illness. Then the shunned realization came, made him stand up as though he were an intruder. On this cot, or perhaps the one across the room, he had made love to Lydia—that spring, the first and only time before their marriage. In August, she had discovered that she was pregnant. Gordon had never for a moment given them cause to regret that inducement to marriage. But Lydia's cautionary approach to sexual relations had made Gordon an only child.

Glancing around the room he hoped to discover a picture of himself. Seeing none, he sat down again. Under his thumb, he felt a rough texture on the wooden frame of the cot. The cigarette burn he had made himself in 1945. Then *this* had been Gordon's cot. Of course. By his desk. Flinging back the sheets, Ernest found nothing.

He crossed the room to Carter's cot where a dimestore reproduction of a famous painting of Jesus hung on the wall. Jerking hard to unstick the sheets, he lay bare Carter's bed. Twisted white sweat socks at the bottom. He shook them out. Much too large for Gordon. But Carter, then Gordon, had worn them with Carter's cowboy boots. Gordon had been sleeping in Carter's bed. Pressing one knee against the edge of the cot, Ernest leaned over and pushed his palms against the wall to examine closely what it was that had disturbed him about the painting. Tiny holes like acne scars in Jesus' upturned face. Ernest looked up. Ragged, feathered darts hung like bats from the ceiling. Someone had printed in Gothic script on the bottom white border: J. C. BLOWS. Using his fingernails, Ernest scraped at the edge of the tape, pulled carefully, but white wall paint chipped off, exposing the wallpaper design that dated back to his own life in the room. He stopped, aware that he had only started his search, that if he took this painting, he might be inclined to take other things. His intention, he stressed again to himself, was only to investigate, to be forewarned, not to search and destroy. But already he had the beer carton containing Carter's, or Gordon's, tee shirt and his own handkerchief to dispose of. He let the picture hang, one edge curling over, obscuring the lettering.

Backing into the center of the room, one leg painfully asleep, Ernest looked at the life-sized girl stuck to the wall with masking tape, holding a banjo over her vagina, the neck of it between her breasts, tip of her tongue touching one of the tuning knobs. His eye on a sticker stuck to the pane, he went to the window again: FRUIT OF THE LOOM. 100% VIRGIN COTTON. More buttons forced him to read: WAR IS GOOD BUSINESS, INVEST YOUR SON. How would the police separate Carter's from Gordon's things? FLOWER POWER. He would simply tell them that Carter had left his junk behind when he bolted. But Gordon's failure to discard some of it, at least the most offensive items, bewildered Ernest. One thing appeared clear: living daily since January among Carter's possessions, Gordon had worn Carter's clothes, slept in Carter's bed.

From the ceiling above the four corners of the room hung the blank faces of four amplifiers, dark mouths gaping. Big Brother is listening. 1984. Late Show. Science fiction bored Ernest. Squatting, he flipped through rec-

ords leaning in a Sunkist orange crate: MILES DAVIS/ THE
GRATEFUL DEAD/ LEADBELLY/ THE BEATLES, their picture
red x-ed out/ MANTOVANI/ THE MAMAS AND THE PAPAS/
THE LOVING SPOONFUL. He was wasting time—Carter's
records couldn't be used against Gordon. But then he
found Glenn Miller's "In the Mood" and "Moonlight
Serenade," a 78-rpm collector's item he had given Gordon. "Soothing background music for test-cramming
time." TOM PAXTON/ THE MOTHERS OF INVENTION/ 1812
OVERTURE (Gordon's?)/ THE ELECTRONIC ERA/ JOAN
BAEZ/ CHARLIE PARKER/ BARTOK.

Rising, he saw a poster he had not glimpsed before,
stuck to the wall with a bowie knife, curled inward at its
four corners: a color photograph of a real banana rising
like a finger out of the middle of a cartoon fist.

Over the rolltop desk hung a guitar, its mouth crammed
full of wilted roses. The vomit taste in his own mouth
made Ernest retch. Hoping Carter had left some whiskey
behind, he quickly searched the rolltop desk, and found
a Jack Daniel's bottle in one of the cubbyholes. Had Gordon taken the last swallow himself this morning just before stepping out of this room?

Finding a single cigarette in a twisted package, Ernest
lit it, quickly snuffed it in a hubcap used as an ashtray.
The smell of fresh smoke would make the police suspi-
cious. Recent daily activity had left Carter's desk a sham-
bles. Across the room, Gordon's desk was merely a sur-
face, strewn with junk. The Royal portable typewriter
he had given Gordon for Christmas his freshman year sat
on Carter's desk, the capital lock key set.

Among the papers on Carter's desk, Ernest searched for
Gordon's notes for his speech. Ernest had been awed by
the way Gordon prepared his senior project in high

school—very carefully, starting with an outline, going through three versions, using cards, dividers, producing a forty-page research paper on Wordsworth. Lydia had said, "Why Ernest, he's been that way since junior high, worrying about college." On Carter's desk, Ernest found the beginnings of papers on Dryden, *The Iliad, Huckleberry Finn.* While he had always felt contentment in Gordon's perfect social behavior and exemplary academic conduct and achievements, sustained from grammar school right on through college, Ernest had sometimes felt, but quickly dismissed, a certain dismay. In her presence, Ernest agreed with Lydia's objections to Gordon's desire to major in English, but alone with him, he had told Gordon, "Satisfy yourself first of all." But he couldn't tell Gordon that he had pretended to agree with his mother to prevent her from exaggerating her suspicion that their marriage had kept him from switching to English himself after he got his B.S. in Business Administration. Each time she brought up the subject, Ernest wondered for weeks what his life would have been like had he become an English professor. As he hastily surveyed the contents of the desk, he felt the absence of the papers Gordon had written that had earned A's, helping to qualify him, as the student with the highest honors, to give the valedictory address.

Handling chewed pencils made Ernest sense the taste of lead and wood on his own tongue. He noticed a CORN FLAKES box but was distracted by a ball-point pen that only great force could have thrust so firmly into the oak desk. The buffalo side of a worn nickel leaned against a bright Kennedy half-dollar. Somewhere under this floor lay a buffalo nickel he had lost himself through a crack. Perhaps Gordon or Carter had found it. He unfolded a

letter. It thanked Carter for his two-hundred-dollar con-
tribution to a legal defense fund for students who had
gone, without permission, to Cuba. Pulling another letter out of a pigeonhole, he discovered a bright gold piece
resembling a medal. Trojan contraceptive. His own
brand before Lydia became bedridden. Impression of it
still on his wallet—no, that was the *old* wallet he carried
as a senior. The letter thanked Carter for his inquiry about
summer work with an organization sponsored by
SNCC. In another pigeonhole, he found a letter outlining
Carter's duties during a summer voter campaign in Mis-
sissippi. "As for the friend you mention, we don't believe
it would be in our best interests to attempt to persuade
him to join in our work. If persuasion is desirable, who
is more strategically situated than you, his own roommate?" Marginal scrawl in pencil: "This is the *man* talking, Baby!"

As he rifled through the numerous letters, folded hastily and slipped or stuffed into pigeonholes, Ernest felt he
was getting an overview of liberal and left-wing activities,
mostly student-oriented, over the past five years, for Carter's associations began in high school. He lifted his elbow
off Gordon's scrapbook—birthday present from Lydia—
and flipped through it. Newspaper photo of students at
a rally, red ink enringing a blurred head, a raised fist.
Half full: clippings of Carter's activities. AP photo: Carter, bearded, burning his draft card. But no creep—
handsome, hair and smile like Errol Flynn in "The Sea
Hawk." Looking around at the poster photograph he
hadn't recognized when he came in, Ernest saw Carter,
wearing a Gestapo billcap, a monocle, an opera cape,
black tights, Zorro boots, carrying a riding crop. When
Ernest first noticed the ads—"Blow Yourself Up"—he

had thought it a good deal at $2.99. Had Gordon given the scrapbook to Carter, or had he cut and pasted the items himself?

Ernest shoved the scrapbook aside and reached for a letter. "Gordy, This is just to tell you to save your tears over King. We all wept over JFK our senior year in high school, and we haven't seen straight since. King just wasn't where the action's at. Okay, so I told you different a few months ago! How come you're always light years behind *me*? Catch up! Make the leap! I'm dumping all these creeps that try to play a rigged game. Look at Robert! I think I'm beginning to understand Oswald and Speck and Whitman. They're the *real* individuals! They work alone while we run together like zebras. But, on the other hand, maybe the same cat did *all* those jobs. And maybe Carter knows who. Sleep on *that* one, Gordy, Baby." Boot camp. April 5. Suddenly, the first day back from Christmas vacation, Carter had impulsively walked out of this room. "See America first! Then the world!" That much Gordon had told them when Ernest and Lydia telephoned at Easter, made uneasy by his terse letter informing them that he was remaining on campus to "watch the locusts emerge from their seventeen-year buried infancy into appalling one-week adulthood," adding, parenthetically, that he had to finish his honors project. Marriage to Lydia had prevented Ernest's desire, like Carter's, to see the world. Not "prevented." Postponed perhaps. A vice-president of a large insurance company might hope to make such a dream come true—if only after he retired. Deep in a pigeonhole, Ernest found a snapshot of Gordon, costumed for a part in *Tom Sawyer*— one of the kids who saunter by in the whitewashing scene.

False freckles. He had forgotten. On the back, tabs of fuzzy black paper—ripped out of the scrapbook.

Mixed in with Carter's were Lydia's letters. "Gordon Precious, You promised—" Feverish eyes. Bed rashes. Blue Cross. Solitude. Solitaire. "Sleep, Lydia." Finding none of his own letters, Ernest remembered writing last week from his office, and the sense of solitude on the fifteenth floor, where he had seemed the only person stirring, came back momentarily. Perhaps in some drawer or secret compartment all his letters to Gordon (few though they had been) and perhaps other little mementos—his sharp-shooter's medal and the Korean coin that he had given Gordon, relics of his three years in the service, and matchbooks from the motels where he and Gordon had stayed on occasional weekend trips—were stored. Surely, somewhere in the room, he would turn up a picture of himself. He had always known that Gordon preferred his mother, but had he conscientiously excluded his father from his life, eliminating all trace? No, he shouldn't jump to conclusions. He had yet to gather and analyze all the evidence. Thinking in those terms about what he was doing, Ernest realized that not only was he going to destroy evidence to protect Gordon's memory as much as possible and shield Lydia, he was now deliberately searching for fragments of a new Gordon, hoping to know and understand him, each discovery destroying the old Gordon who would now always remain a stranger.

But he didn't have time to move so slowly, like a slow-motion movie. Turning quickly in Carter's swivel chair, Ernest bent over the large CORN FLAKES box, brimful of papers that had been dropped, perhaps tossed, into it. Gordon's themes, including his honors thesis in a stiff black binder: "ANGUISH, SPIRITUAL AND PHYSICAL IN GERARD MANLEY HOPKINS' POETRY. Approved by: Alfred Hansen, Thorne Halpert (who had come to Melbourne in Ernest's own freshman year), Richard Kelp, John Morton." In red pencil at the bottom, haphazard scrawls, as if they were four different afterthoughts: "*Dis*approved by: Jason Carter, Gordon Foster, Lydia Foster, Gerard Manley Hopkins." Up the left margin, in lead pencil: "PISS ON *ALL* OF YOU!" Ernest saw Gordon burning the box in the community dump on the edge of the village.

Ernest stepped over to Gordon's desk, seeking some sort of perspective, some evidence of Gordon's life before he moved over to the rolltop desk and mingled his own things with Carter's. The gray steel drawers were empty. Not just empty. Clean. Wiped clean with a rag—a swipe in the middle drawer had dried in a soapy pattern of broken beads of moisture. Ernest saw there an image: a clean table that made him feel the presence behind him of another table where Gordon now, in pieces, lay. Under dirty clothes slung aside lay stacks of books and old newspapers, whose headlines of war, riot, murder, assassinations, negotiations seemed oddly remote in this room. The portable tape recorder Ernest had given Gordon last fall to help him through his senior year. He pressed the LISTEN button. Nothing. He pressed the REWIND. LISTEN. ". . . defy analysis. But let's examine this passage from Aristotle's 'De Interpretatione': 'In the case of that which is or which has taken place, propositions, whether positive or negative, must be true or false.' " "What did he say?" Someone whispering. "I didn't catch it." (Gordon's voice?) "Again, in the case of a pair of contraries—

contradictories, that is. . . ." The professor's voice slipped into a fizzing silence. "I'm recording your speech, son," he had written to Gordon last week, "so your mother can hear it." But Ernest had forgotten his tape recorder.

The headline of a newspaper announced Charlie Whitman's sniper slaying of twelve people from the observation tower of the University administration building in Austin, Texas. But that was two summers past. Melbourne had no summer school. Folded, as though mailed. Had Carter sent it to Gordon from—Where *was* Carter from? Had Gordon received it at home?

A front page news photo showed a Buddhist monk burning on a Saigon street corner. Ernest's sneer faded in bewilderment as he saw that the caption identified an American woman burning on the steps of the Pentagon. Smudged pencil across the flames: THE MOTHER OF US ALL. Children bereft, left to a father, perhaps no father even. Ernest tried to remember the name of one of his clients, an English professor, who shot himself a week after the assassination of Martin Luther King. No note. Any connection? His wife showed Ernest the Student Guide to Courses—one anonymous, thus sexless, student's evaluation might have been a contributing factor: "This has got to be the most boring human being on the face of the earth." Since then, Ernest had tried to make his own presentations at company meetings more entertaining. Lately, many cases of middle-aged men who had mysteriously committed suicide hovered on the periphery of Ernest's consciousness. It struck him now that in every case, he had forgotten most of the "sensible" explanations, leaving nothing but mystery. Wondering whether those men had seen something in the eyes of their children, even their wives, that Ernest himself had been blind to, he shuddered but did not shake off a sudden clenching of muscles in his shoulders. "When the cause of death is legally ruled as suicide," he had often written, "the company is relieved of its obligations to—" Did Gordon *know* the grenade would explode? Or did he borrow it, perhaps steal it from a museum, and then did it, like the locusts, seventeen years dormant, suddenly come alive? Ernest had always been lukewarm about gun controls, but now he would insist on a thorough investigation to determine where Gordon purchased the grenade. Dealer in war surplus? Could they *prove* he meant it to go off? "When the cause of death is legally ruled—" Horrified that he was thinking so reflexively like an insurance executive, Ernest slammed his fist into his groin, and staggered back into the bed Gordon had abandoned.

His eyes half-opened, he saw his cigarette burn again on the wooden frame beside his hand. He recalled Gordon's vivid letter home the first week of his freshman year: "My roommate turns my stomach by the way he dresses, talks, acts, eats, sleeps." Ernest had thought that a boy so different from Gordon would be good for him, so his efforts, made at Lydia's fretful urgings, to have Carter replaced, or to have Gordon moved, were slapdash. He very much wanted his son to go through Melbourne in his old room. Books on Gordon's desk at the foot of the cot caught his attention. Some dating from junior high, these were all Gordon's, including the Great Books, with their marvelous Syntopicon. As the swelling pain in his groin subsided, Ernest stood up, hovered over the books.

A frayed copy of *Winnie the Pooh* startled him. "To Ernest, Christmas, 1928. All my love, Grandmother."

The year he learned to write, Gordon had printed his own name in green crayon across the top of the next page. As Ernest leafed through the book, nostalgia eased his nerves. Penciled onto Winnie the Pooh was a gigantic penis extending across the page to Christopher Robin, who was bending over a daisy. "Damn you, Carter!" Ernest slammed it down—a pillar of books slurred, tumbled onto the floor. He stood still, staring into the green light, trying to detect the voices of people who might have heard in the rooms below. Ernest heard only the locusts in the light. A newspaper that had fallen leaned and sagged like a tent: Whitman's face looked up from the floor, two teeth in his high school graduation smile blacked out, a pencil-drawn tongue flopping out of his mouth. His name was scratched out and YOU AND ME, BABY was lettered in. Ernest kicked at the newspaper, twisted his heel into Whitman's face, and the paper rose up around his ankles like a yellowed flower, soot-dappled.

Ernest backed into the swivel chair, turned, rested his head in his hands on the rolltop desk, and breathed in fits and starts. He wanted to throw the hubcap ashtray through the stained-glass window and feel the spring air rush in upon his face and fill and stretch his lungs. Cigarillo butts, scorched Robert Burns bands, cigarette butts. Marijuana? He sniffed, but realized he couldn't recognize it if it *were*.

Was there nothing in the room but pale emanations of Carter's gradual transformation of Gordon? Closing his eyes, trying to conjure up Gordon's face, he saw, clearly, only Carter's smile, like a weapon, in the draft-card-burning photograph. *Wanting* to understand Gordon, he had only a shrill scream of defiance, an explosion, and this littered room with which to begin. He imagined the mortician, fitting pieces together, an arm on a drain board behind him. And when he was finished, what would he have accomplished? In the explosion, Gordon had vacated his body, and now the pieces had stopped moving, but the objects in his room twitched when Ernest touched them. Taking a deep breath, he inhaled the stench of spit and tobacco. He shoved the hubcap aside, and stood up.

Bending his head sideways, mashing his ear against his shoulder, Ernest read the titles of books crammed into cinderblock and pineboard shelves between Carter's cot and the window: 120 DAYS OF SODOM, the Marquis de Sade/ AUTOBIOGRAPHY OF MALCOLM X/THE POSTMAN ALWAYS RINGS TWICE, James M. Cain/MEIN KAMPF—. He caught himself reading titles and authors aloud in a stupor. Silently, his lips still moving, he read: BOY SCOUT HANDBOOK. Though he had never been a scout, Ernest had agreed with Lydia that, like a fraternity, it would be good for Gordon in future life. FREEDOM NOW, Max Reiner/ NAUSEA, Jean-Paul Sartre/ ATLAS SHRUGGED, Ayn Rand/ THE SCARLET LETTER. Heritage, leather-bound edition he had given Gordon for his sixteenth birthday. He had broken in the new Volkswagen, a surprise graduation present, driving it down. Late for the ceremonies, he had parked it, illegally, behind De-Lozier Hall so it would be there when he and Gordon brought the suitcases and his other belongings down. CASTRO'S CAUSE, Harvey Kreyborg/ NOTES FROM UNDERGROUND, Dostoyevski:/ LADY CHATTERLEY'S LOVER, Ernest's own copy. Had Gordon sneaked it out of the house? Slumping to his knees, he squinted at titles he had been unable to make out: Carter had cynically shelved Ernest's own copy of PROFILES IN COURAGE, passed on to Gordon, next to OSWALD RESURRECTED by Eugene Federogh.

There was a book with a library number on its spine. He would have to return that. The Gordon he had known would have done so before commencement. Afraid the police might come in suddenly and catch him there, Ernest rose to his feet. Glancing through several passages, highlighted with a yellow magic-marker, he realized that he was reading about "anguish, spiritual and physical, in Gerard Manley Hopkins' poetry." He rooted through the CORN FLAKES box again, took out Gordon's honors thesis. Flipping through the pages, he discovered a passage that duplicated, verbatim, a marked passage in the book. No footnote reference. The bibliography failed to cite the book that he held in his hand and now let drop, along with the honors thesis, into the beer carton onto Carter's fouled tee shirt and Ernest's handkerchief.

Why had he cheated? He never had before. Or had he plagiarized *all* those papers, from junior high on up to this one? No, surely, this time only. Ernest himself had felt the pressure in his senior year, and most of the boys in his fraternity had cheated when they really *had* to. Now he felt compelled to search thoroughly, examine everything carefully. The police had no right to invade a dead boy's privacy and plunge his invalid mother into grief.

In Carter's desk drawers, Ernest searched more systematically among letters and notes, still expecting to discover an early draft of Gordon's unfinished speech; perhaps it would be full of clues. He might even find the bill of sale for the grenade. Across the naked belly of a girl ripped from a magazine was written: "Gordy—" Carter had even renamed, rechristened Gordon. "Jeff and Conley and I are holding a peace vigil in the cold rain tonight, all night. Bring us a fresh jar of water at midnight. And leave your goddamn middle-class mottos in the room. Love, Carter."

A letter from Fort Jackson, South Carolina, April 20, 1968. "Dear Gordon, I am being shipped to Vietnam. I will never see you again. I have not forgotten what you said to me that night in our room across the Dark Gulf between our cots. As always, Carter." Without knowing what Carter meant, Ernest knew that gulf himself. He had tried to bridge it, touch Scott, his own roommate, whose lassitude about life's possibilities often provoked Ernest to wall-pounding rage. He had finally persuaded Scott to take a trip West with him right after graduation. Scott's nonchalant withdrawal at the last minute was so dispiriting that Ernest had accepted his father's offer of a summer internship with the insurance company as a claims adjustor.

A 1967 letter described in detail the march on the Pentagon. "What are you doing down there, you little fink? You should be up here with the rest of us. My brothers have been beaten by the cops. I'm not against the use of napalm in *some* instances. Just don't let me get my hands on any of it when those pig sonofabitches come swinging their sticks at us. We're rising up all over the world, Baby—or didn't you know it, with your nose in Chaucer's tales. Melbourne is about due to be hit so you'd better decide who's side you're on. I heard about this one campus demonstration where somebody set fire to this old fogey's life-long research on some obscure hang-up of his. I can think of a few at Melbourne that need shaking up." Ernest was shocked, then surprised at himself for being shocked. He wondered how Gordon had felt.

As Ernest pulled a postcard out of a pigeonhole, a white capsule rolled out into his hand. For a common cold, or LSD? He stifled an impulse to swallow it. By chance escape what chance might reveal. He flipped the capsule against the inside of the CORN FLAKES box and it popped like a cap pistol. Comic postcard—outhouse, hillbillies—mailed from Alabama, December 12, 1966. "Gordy, Baby, Wish you were here. You sure as hell ain't all *there*! Love, till death do us part, Carter." In several letters, Carter fervently attempted to persuade Gordon to abandon his "middle-class Puritan Upforcing" and embrace the cause of world brotherhood, which itself embraced all other great causes of "our time." But even through the serious ones ran a trace of self-mockery. He found Carter's draft notice, his *own* name crossed out, Gordon's typed in. Across the body of the form letter, dated February 1, 1968, was printed in Gothic script: NON SERVIUM.

As Ernest reached for a bunch of postcards, he realized that he was eager not only to discover more about Gordon, but to assemble into some shape the fragments of Carter's life. A series of postcards with cryptic, taunting messages traced Carter's trail over the landscape of America, from early January to the middle of March, 1968. From Carmel, California, a view of a tower and cypress trees: "Violence is the sire of all the world's values." Ernest remembered the card Gordon sent him from Washington, D.C., when he was in junior high: "Dear Dad, Our class went to see Congress but they were closed. Our teacher got mad. She dragged us all to the Smithsonian and showed us Lindbergh's airplane. It was called THE SPIRIT OF ST. LOUIS. I didn't think it looked so hot. Mrs. Landis said she saved the headlines when she was in high school. Did you? Your son, Gordon."

Ernest found a night letter from Lynn, Massachusetts. "Dear Gordon, Remembering that Jason spoke of you so often and so fondly, his father and I felt certain that you would not want to learn through the newspapers that our dear son has been reported missing in action. While no one can really approve in his heart of this war, Jason has always been the sort of boy who believed in dying for his convictions. We know that you will miss him. He loved you as though you were his own brother. Affectionate regards, Grace and Harold Carter." June 1, 1968, three days ago.

Trembling, Ernest sought more letters from Carter. One from boot camp summed up, in wild, impassioned prose, Carter's opinions on civil rights, the war, and "the American Dream that's turned into a nightmare." In another, "God is dead and buried on LBJ's ranch" dispensed with religion and politics, "inseparable." May 4, 1968: "Dear Gordy, We are in the jungle now, on a search and destroy mission. You have to admire some of these platoon leaders. I must admit I enjoy watching them act out their roles as all-American tough guys. They have a kind of style, anyway. In here you don't have time to analyze your thoughts. But I just thought a word or two written at the scene of battle might bring you the smell of smoke." Ernest sniffed the letter, uncertain whether the faint smell came from the paper.

He pulled a wadded letter out of a pigeonhole where someone had stuffed it. As he unwadded the note, vicious ball-point pen markings wove a mesh over the words: "Gordon, I'm moving in with Conley. Pack my things and set them in the hall. I don't even want to *enter* that room again. What you said last night made me sick. I've lived with you for three and a half years because I was always convinced that I could save your soul. But after last night, I know it's hopeless. Carter." Across the "Dark Gulf" between their beds, what could *Gordon* have said to shock Carter? Had Gordon persuaded him to stay after all? Or was it the next day that Carter had "impulsively" run away? Ernest searched quickly through the rest of the papers, hoping no answer existed, but knowing that if one did and he failed to find it, the police wouldn't fail.

"Gordy, Baby, Everything you read is lies! I've been in the field three weeks now. My whole life's search ends here, in this burning village, where I'm taking time to write to you. Listen, Baby, this is life! This is what it's all about. In the past weeks I've personally set fire to thirty-seven huts belonging to Viet Cong sympathizers. Don't listen to those sons-of-bitches who whine and gripe and piss and moan about this war. This is a *just* war. We're on the right side, man, the *right* side. This place has opened my eyes and heart, baby. With the bullets and the blood all around, you see things clearer. Words! To hell with words! All these beady-eyed little bastards understand is *bullets*, and a knife now and then. These bastards killed my buddy, a Black boy by the name of Bird. The greatest guy that ever lived. Well, there's ten Viet Cong that ain't alive today because of what they did to my buddy, and there'll be another hundred less Viet Cong if I can persuade them to send me out after I'm due to be pulled back. Yesterday, I found a Viet Cong in a hut with his goddamn wife and kids. I turned the flame thrower on the sons-of-bitches and when the hut burned down, I pissed on the hot ashes. I'm telling you all this to open your eyes, mister. This is the way it really is. Join your ass up, get over here where you belong. Forget everything I ever said to you or wrote to you before. I have seen the light. The future of the world will be decided right here. And I will fight until the last Viet Cong is dead. Always, your friend, Carter." May 21, 1968, two weeks ago.

Trying to feel as Gordon had felt reading this letter, feeling nothing, Ernest remembered Gordon's response to a different piece of information some kid in grammar school dealt him when he was eleven. Having informed Gordon that Santa Claus was a lie, he added the observation that nobody ever knows who his real father and mother are. Just as Ernest stepped into the house from the office, Gordon had asked: "Are you my real father?" In the living room where colored lights blazed on the tree, Lydia was weeping. It took two months to rid Gordon of the fantasy that he had been adopted. Or had he simply stopped interrogating them? But how did a man know *any*thing? Did that professor ever suspect that one day in print he would be labeled "the most boring man on the face of the earth"? Did Carter ever sense he would end up killing men in Vietnam? Did Gordon ever suspect that on his graduation day...?

Now the day began to make sense. After Carter's letter from Vietnam, reversing everything he had preached to Gordon, Gordon had let his studies slide, and then the plagiarism had just happened, the way things will, because how could he really care anymore? Then did the night letter from Carter's mother shock him into pulling the grenade pin? Was "I advocate a total revolution!" Gordon's *own* climax to the attitude expressed in Carter's Vietnam letter? Or did the *old* Carter finally speak through Gordon's mouth? These possibilities made sense, but Ernest felt nothing.

His foot kicked a metal wastebasket under Carter's desk. Squatting, he pulled it out, and sitting again in the swivel chair, began to unwad several letters. "Dear

Dad—" The rest blank. "Dead Dad—" Blank. "Dear Dad—" Blank. "Dear Father—" Blank. "Dear Dad—" Blank.

Ernest swung around in Carter's chair, rocked once, got to his feet, stood in the middle of the room, his hands dangling in front of him, the leaded moldings of the window cast black wavy lines over his suit, the green light stained his hands, his heart beat so fast he became aware that he was panting. Like a dog. His throat felt dry, his tongue swollen, eyes burning from reading in the oblique light. Dark spots of sweat on the floor. "Gordon. Gordon. Gordon."

Whatever Gordon had said in his valedictory address, Ernest knew that certain things in this room would give the public the wrong image of his son. Or perhaps—he faced it—the right image. Wrong or right, it would incite the disease in Lydia's body to riot and she would burn. He rolled the desk top down and began stuffing things into the beer carton. When it was full, he emptied the contents of the CORN FLAKES box onto the desk, throwing only the honors thesis back into it. When he jerked the bowie knife out of the wall, the banana poster fell. He scraped at the clotting vomit on the clothes hanging in the closet, and wiped the blade on the sole of his shoe. Then he filled the CORN FLAKES box with letters and other incriminating objects.

He opened the door and looked out. The hall was dim and deserted. The surviving seniors had gone home, though some must have lingered behind with wounded classmates, teachers, parents. The police would still be occupied with traffic. The back staircase was dark. He stacked the beer carton on top of the CORN FLAKES box, lifted both in his arms, and started to back out the door. But under the rolltop desk in a bed of lint lay a piece of paper that, even wadded up, resembled a telegram. Setting the boxes down, the cardboard already dark brown where he had pressed his forehead, Ernest got on his knees and reached under the desk. Without rising, he unwadded the paper. URGENT YOU RENEW SUBSCRIPTION TO TIME AT STUDENT RATE. STOP. WORLD NEWS AT YOUR FINGERTIPS. STOP. Mock telegram technique, special reply pencil enclosed.

The boxes were heavier as Ernest lifted them again and backed out the door, almost certain that the grenade had not been a rhetorical flourish. Bracing the boxes against the wall, lifting his knee under them, Ernest quickly reached out, pulled at the door knob. When the door slammed, locked, startling him, he grabbed the boxes as they almost tipped over into the stairwell.

He had to descend very slowly. The narrow staircase curved twice before it reached the basement. His shoulder slid along the wall as he went down, carefully, step by step. The bottom of the box cut into his palms, sweat tickled his spine, and his thighs chafed each other as sweat dried on his flesh. He saw nothing until he reached the basement where twilight coming through the window of the door revealed the furnace. As he fumbled for the doorknob, already the devouring locusts jangled in his ears like a single note quivering relentlessly on a violin.

Locusts had dropped from the ivy onto the black hood of the Volkswagen, parked up tight against the building. He opened the trunk, set the boxes inside, closed the lid, locked it.

As he got in behind the wheel, a glimpse of the cemetery behind the dormitory made him recall the grave that had so awed him during his freshman year. From where he sat, turning the ignition key, the larger tombs of the historic dead obscured the small white stone, but he had not forgotten the epitaph: HERE LIES AN UNIDENTIFIED VICTIM OF THE FIRE THAT RAZED DELOZIER HALL, May 16, 1938. Since all the Melbourne students had been accounted for, he (or perhaps she) must have been a visitor.

Pulling off the highway, he drove along a dirt trail, new grass sprouting between the wheel ruts. Here, as visible evidence testified, Melbourne students brought the girls who came down from Briarheath. Parked, he let dusk turn to dark.

Then he left the woods, lights dimmed until he got onto the highway. On the outskirts of the town, looking at this distance like a village erected in one of those elaborate electric train sets, he turned onto a cinder road and stopped at a gate, got out, lifted the latch, drove through, then went back and closed the gate.

Headlights off, he eased over the soft, sooty dirt road, the rough bushes on each side a soft gray blur, into the main lot, where the faculty and other townspeople dumped junk and garbage.

The smell made him aware of the taste at the back of his mouth, the stench of burning rubber and plastic and dead animals made his headache pound more fiercely, his left eyelid beat like a pulse.

He unlocked the trunk, lifted out the CORN FLAKES box, and stumbled in the dark over tin cans and broken tools and springs and tires, set the box down, then went back and got the other box.

The boxes weren't far enough into the dump. He dragged them, one with each hand, backwards, up and over the rough terrain, stumbling, cutting his hand on rusty cans and nails in charred wood, thinking of tetanus, of Lydia without him.

Standing up, he sucked in the night air, feeling a dewy freshness mingled with the acrid smoke and fumes. He reached into his pocket for his lighter. His thumb began to hurt as he failed repeatedly to make the flint catch.

A bright beam shot out over the dump, another several yards beside it, then another—powerful flashlights—and as he crouched to avoid the lights, rifle fire shattered the silence over the dump. Reaching out, grabbing the cardboard flaps to keep his balance, Ernest squatted beside his boxes.

"Get that son-of-a-bitch, Doc!"

Twisting his neck around, Ernest saw the beam swing and dip through oily smoke coiling out of the debris and stop on a rat, crouched on a fire-blackened icebox door. It started to run. But the slick porcelain allowed its feet no traction.

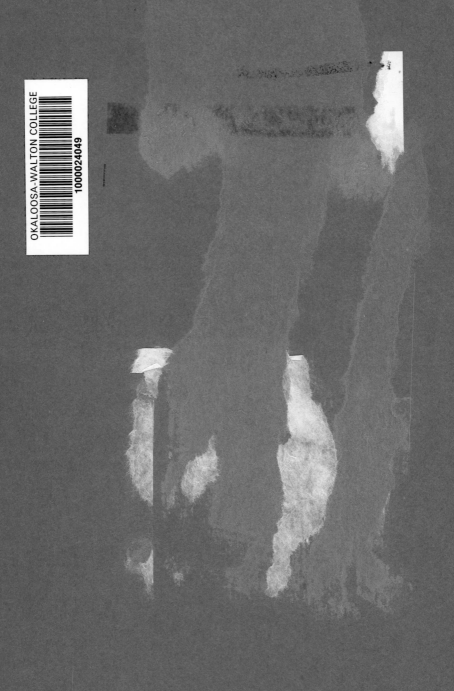